He turned to look at her—even more stunning than she'd been a couple of hours before when he'd married her. If that were possible...

"Reed?" Alcina asked. "What's wrong?"

"Nothing. I'm just thinking. Trying to shake the tension of the big day."

Suddenly the moment was here and he was struck dumb. He had to say something to get the ball rolling.

"Don't worry. I won't let anything interfere with my... uh...my husbandly duties."

She laughed. "Your what?"

"I know we both think of this marriage as a kind of business deal, but—"

"But what?" she asked, her amusement vanishing. "Are you saying that you're willing to put yourself out to seal the deal, so to speak?"

Heck, he'd gone and said the exact wrong thing. He'd never been good with fancy words. He was better at doing. Stepping toward Alcina, he slipped his arms around her back and brushed her lips with his.

"You're my wife now," he said simply. "And we both have our...physical needs...."

Dear Harlequin Intrigue Reader,

The thrills never stop at Harlequin Intrigue. This month, get geared up for danger and desire in double helpings!

There's something about a mysterious man that makes him all the more appealing. In *The Silent Witness* (#565), Alex Coughlin is just such a man on assignment and undercover. But can he conceal his true feelings for Nicki Michaels long enough to catch a killer? Join Dani Sinclair and find out as she returns to FOOLS POINT.

The search for the truth is Clay Jackson's only focus—until he learns the woman he never stopped loving was keeping the biggest secret of all...a baby. See why *Intimate Secrets* (#566) are the deepest with author B.J. Daniels.

Patricia Rosemoor winds up her SONS OF SILVER SPRINGS miniseries this month. Reed is the last Quarrels brother to go the way of the altar as he enters a marriage of convenience with the one woman he thought he'd never have, in *A Rancher's Vow* (#567).

Finally, welcome multitalented author Jo Leigh as she contributes her first Harlequin Intrigue title, *Little Girl Found* (#568). She also begins a three-month bonanza of books! Look for her titles from Harlequin American Romance (June) and Harlequin Temptation (July). You won't be sorry.

Gripping tales of mystery, suspense that never lets up and sizzling romance to boot. Pick up all four titles for the total Harlequin Intrigue experience.

Sincerely,

Denise O'Sullivan
Associate Senior Editor
Harlequin Intrigue

A Rancher's Vow
Patricia Rosemoor

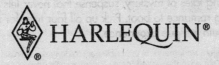

HARLEQUIN®

TORONTO • NEW YORK • LONDON
AMSTERDAM • PARIS • SYDNEY • HAMBURG
STOCKHOLM • ATHENS • TOKYO • MILAN • MADRID
PRAGUE • WARSAW • BUDAPEST • AUCKLAND

ISBN 0-373-22567-9

A RANCHER'S VOW

This edition published by arrangement with Harlequin Books S.A.

® and TM are trademarks of the publisher. Trademarks indicated with
® are registered in the United States Patent and Trademark Office, the
Canadian Trade Marks Office and in other countries.

Visit us at www.eHarlequin.com

Printed in U.S.A.

ABOUT THE AUTHOR

Patricia Rosemoor is the recipient of the 1997 Career Achievement Award in Romantic Suspense from *Romantic Times Magazine*.

To research her novels, Patricia is willing to swim with dolphins, round up mustangs or howl with wolves. "Whatever it takes to write a credible tale," she says. She even went to jail for a day—as a guest of Cook County—to research a proposal.

Ms. Rosemoor holds a Master of Television degree and a B.A. in American literature from the University of Illinois. She lives in Chicago with her husband, Edward, and their three cats.

Books by Patricia Rosemoor

HARLEQUIN INTRIGUE

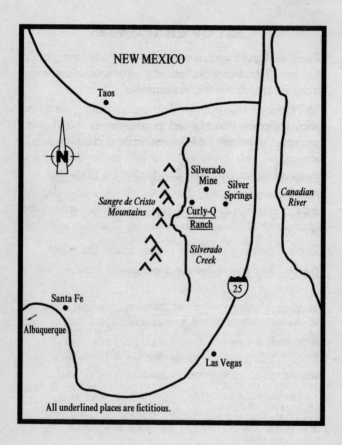

NEW MEXICO

Taos

N

Sangre de Cristo
Mountains

Silverado
Mine

Silver
Springs

Curly-Q
Ranch

Silverado
Creek

Canadian
River

25

Santa Fe

Albuquerque

Las Vegas

All underlined places are fictitious.

CAST OF CHARACTERS

Reed Quarrels — He would do anything to save the ranch and win his father's approval, even if it meant marrying the daughter of his father's nemesis.

Alcina Dale — She agreed to a business arrangement with Reed, because she'd always loved him.

Emmett Quarrels — His manipulations were for naught this time.

Tucker Dale — His search for the truth led to danger.

Reba Gantry — The café owner knew too much.

Cesar Cardona — The developer was looking for his next land acquisition.

Vernon Martell — The neighboring rancher had no scruples when it came to increasing the size of his spread.

Hugh Ruskin — The bartender knew more than he should about everyone in town.

To my editor, Angela Catalano, for her patience
and understanding.

Thanks to my writing friends who went beyond the
call of duty and got me where I needed to be—
Catherine Andorka, Sherrill Bodine, Arlene Erlbach,
Cheryl Jefferson, Jody Lowenthal, Jude Mandell,
Sue Myers, Rosemary Paulas and Elaine Sima.

And special thanks to Linda Sweeney for jogging
my brain when it stalled out.

Prologue

For a moment, he glanced at Prudence Prescott Quarrels, who did look beautiful, he supposed, as all brides should on their wedding day.

"Congratulations!" He slapped the groom on the back. "You have yourself some new wife there."

"Thanks." Grinning like an idiot, Chance Quarrels pumped his hand. "I think so, too."

"So what are your plans? Where are you gonna settle down?"

"Right here on the Curly-Q, of course."

"Hmm. I thought your pa had a full house right now, with your brother Bart and his kids."

"We'll be staying with Pru's sister until we work something out." Chance was obviously distracted. "Listen, I'd better get back to Pru before she accuses me of deserting her again."

"You go on then."

Smiling to himself, he watched the unsuspecting cowboy hurry to his new wife's side—he was a fool in love with no thoughts but those prompted by his youthful libido.

They would all be unsuspecting today, he knew, looking around at the crowd of more than a hundred. A day of celebration. Of giving thanks.

No one would be thankful before the night ended, however. He'd see to that.

He chuckled to himself as he moved to his vehicle through the knots of relatives and friends and neighbors, well-wishers all. They were also lambs, so to speak, without a suspicious thought in their heads.

And why should there be any doubt-sayers on such a glorious mid-November day?

He swept his gaze over the grounds until he found his real quarry. Emmett Quarrels. Look at him smiling, puffing out his chest in pride...

The fear of God had not been put into the old man yet. Unbelievable as it seemed, Quarrels was not getting the message that his situation was serious.

This message would be closer to home and delivered right under his nose. Under *everyone's* noses. He'd be right in their midst and no one would be able to point a finger his way. No one would even suspect him.

That was the beauty of his plan.

From the back of his vehicle, he dug out the special wedding present that he'd hidden under a tarp and strolled along the buildings with the elegantly wrapped package tucked under one arm. No one even looked at him twice.

A very unique wedding present, indeed, he thought with a wry laugh.

They'd all get a blast out of it later.

Chapter One

The dog's eyes no longer held suspicion when they gazed at him, but still she remained curled on the floor, shoulder wedged against the passenger seat, as Reed Quarrels pulled his truck onto the washboard dirt road that signaled the start of Curly-Q land.

He soon stopped, hopped out and swung open the metal pipe-and-wire gate to his past.

The dog limped along behind him and stopped to sniff around a twisted cypress. Reed didn't rush her. Who knew how long she'd been starving and sick and wounded. He didn't mind giving her a few minutes of privacy.

Fetching a jug of water from the back of the truck, Reed poured himself a cup. He took a long swallow and looked out over the New Mexican land he hadn't seen in more than a year and which, a lifetime ago, he had mistakenly assumed would be his to run. He'd smartened up more than a dozen years ago, though, and had gone his own way.

Worn cedar and barbed-wire fences surrounded yellowing grasses. A handful of mostly white-faced cattle grazed nearby, and there were more, he knew, in the canyon below. Nearly sixty thousand acres of rich, volcanic-based grasslands as far as the eye could see were broken down into manageable, gated pastures. Reed swept his gaze over the high desert country—almost seven thousand feet—across the long-deserted mining area in the foothills, to the Sangre de Cristo Mountains in the distance.

Closer—only a few feet away—the dog was staring at him expectantly. Reed refilled the cup and, hunkering down to her level, held it out. Her pointed nose dipped into the water, but her gaze never left his face.

"You trust me a little, huh?" he murmured.

In answer, her tail moved slightly, an imitation of a real wag.

"Poor girl." He stared at her ragged, infected ear and only hoped she would trust him enough to let him take care of it later. He hadn't tried touching her yet. "You've had a rough time, haven't you? But your luck just changed. You can count on me to take care of things."

Despite the hamburger he'd bought her earlier, the dog had a hungry look that he figured would stay with her a spell. So he fetched a piece of jerky from his jeans jacket. She practically swallowed it whole.

"That'll have to do you for a little while. Shouldn't eat too much all at once anyhow. You'd be sick."

He rose and moved toward the pickup. The dog jumped in ahead of him and settled back on the floor. She'd ridden there all the way from the truck stop where he'd found her. Not that she'd come to him right off—she'd been terrified and he'd had to wait her out—the reason he'd missed his own brother's wedding. Well, the ceremony, anyway, the celebration was undoubtedly just starting.

Or was the dog an excuse?

If not the dog, would he have found another reason to delay his homecoming?

Not because of Chance, though...

Reed moved the pickup to the other side of the fence, got out, closed the gate and clambered back behind the wheel, a ritual to be repeated all over the large ranch.

Howard Siles had summoned him in person. Pa's lawyer had located all three of the Quarrels boys— each the sole fruit of one of Emmett Quarrels's three disastrous marriages. The lawyer had given Reed the good news-bad news that had cut past his reluctance to bring him home.

The Curly-Q had been turned into a family corporation because Emmett Quarrels was dying.

Pa dying...

Reed could hardly believe it. The old man was too ornery to die.

But Chance was back. And Bart. Reed had called the ranch and had talked to his older half brother the week before only to learn that life on the spread wasn't rosy. Lots of *bad-luck incidents,* as Pa liked to call them, one after the other, and the Curly-Q was broke, the mortgage in arrears.

Bart hadn't elaborated, but Reed was uneasy, nevertheless. A sense of doom which he tried shaking away, hung over his head. The old feelings were crowding him, nothing more. He needn't allow his imagination to run away with him over a couple of accidents.

So why didn't he feel more relaxed?

The pickup lumbered past the scale house where cattle on the way to market would be weighed before being shipped off to auction. No cows or calves in the corral now, Reed noted. He hoped the calves hadn't all been sold off. Beef prices were too damn low. They'd undoubtedly get more per pound in the spring, and the calves would be yearlings and weigh a lot more, as well. They were lucky that the heart of the protected canyon was prime grazing land, even in winter.

Reaching the piñon and ponderosa pine–limned rimrock, the road dotted with dark green cedar, rusting scrub oak and grayish juniper bush, Reed started the descent into the canyon cut by Silverado Creek, which twisted and turned and rushed across the Curly-Q. The vehicle dipped and bounced its way down hairpin curves, while red dust swirled around him.

The buildings spread out below, and beyond them, people spread out like a colony of ants. The wedding celebration was in progress.

As if nothing were wrong…

Things *were* wrong or he and his brothers wouldn't have been summoned home, and Reed knew in his gut that the wrong went beyond Pa's illness. If things didn't come together right quick, the Curly-Q would be a thing of the past. But Bart was a lawman at heart, and Chance had been content alternating between day work and rodeoing for years. *He* was the only one who'd ranched all his life.

Now that Pa was incapacitated, Reed figured that without *him*, the spread would fast go back to desert. Or become part of another ranch. Or be divided and built on—another fancy housing development like that Land of Enchantment Acres he'd seen on the other side of Silver Springs. Ripe pickings for foreigners, he thought. Those southern Californians would move right in.

The Curly-Q needed him.

Pa needed him.

Reed wondered if the old man had figured that out, at last.

HEARING ANOTHER VEHICLE pull up beyond the ranch house, Alcina Dale turned away from Chance and Pru's daughter only for a moment. Chance's twelve-year-old niece, Lainey, had insisted on taking posed photographs of the happy couple before the party began in earnest, and Alcina had volunteered to watch the bride and groom's little redheaded daughter.

And now she was watching for the man who hadn't shown for his own brother's wedding, she realized, chastising her foolish self and quickly returning her attention where it belonged.

Unfortunately, those few seconds of inattention had been more than enough time for the two-year-old to get herself into mischief. The toddler had headed straight to the nearby table that groaned with food for the wedding supper. She was now rocking on tiptoe and reaching both hands high over her head.

"Hope, honey, no!" Alcina cried as the toddler got her fingers on a platter piled with barbecued ribs.

She made a dive for the child as the platter wobbled and a couple of ribs slid off the mound and onto Hope. One slab zapped straight down the front of Alcina's yellow dress that she'd bought to wear as Pru's bridesmaid. Unhurt, Hope shrieked with laughter and lunged for her honorary aunt.

Alcina made her second mistake when she hauled the saucy little girl up into her arms.

"What am I going to do with you?" she asked,

even as Hope laughed again, touching Alcina's face and hair with sticky fingers.

"Maybe we should dunk the little hoyden in the horse trough and be done with it."

This came from a laughing Felice Cuma. The housekeeper set another platter on the table—homemade enchiladas with green sauce. Felice had cooked her heart out for the wedding supper—fried chicken, pork tamales, *posole,* mashed potatoes, beans and more. She'd been the one to insist it be held here on the ranch so she could *do* for Chance, who was as much a son to her as if she'd given birth to him. Alcina knew Chance felt the same sort of love for Felice, who'd raised him after his biological mother had abandoned him.

Felice shook her head as she retrieved the fallen ribs. "Well, the dogs will get a treat," she muttered, carrying the dust-covered meat away from the table and toward the stables where they'd been locked out of the way.

The wedding celebration was being held in the freshly mowed pasture directly behind the sprawling ranch house. A band was setting up by the portable dance floor across the way—once the music got going, everyone would no doubt dance until dark. Not much in the way of entertainment in these parts, Alcina thought, so she was certain the good citizens of Silver Springs would take advantage where they could.

Tables and chairs had been laid out, many under the cottonwoods, but at the moment, most of the hundred or so guests were milling about, getting drinks and talking up a storm. Luckily, the weather was with them. Though it was late November, the sky was a brilliant blue and the afternoon had warmed nearly to seventy.

Alcina was thinking that Chance and Pru couldn't have asked for a more perfect wedding day, when she glanced up into a familiar set of brown eyes that warmed her from the inside.

"Reed," she choked out, the breath catching in her throat, and she realized the vehicle she'd heard *had* been his.

She took a good long look at him. He was wearing creased tan trousers, polished snakeskin boots and a dress shirt buttoned to the throat and held there by a string tie with a jasper catch. He'd filled out some, but he wasn't an imposing man, not like Bart or Chance. Still, he had his own brand of appeal.

"Alcina Dale. It's been a long time," Reed said, the quiet certainty of his voice that she remembered so well thrilling her after all these years.

He removed his pale gray Stetson to reveal neatly combed brown hair. Alcina's mouth went dry. He still reminded her of a young Robert Redford—maybe not as pretty, but modestly handsome in his own right. He had that same dignity as Redford. That same quiet self-assurance.

But as he gave her situation with Hope a once-over, his dignity cracked and he ineffectually tried to smother his laughter with a cough.

Putting an embarrassed Alcina immediately on the defensive.

She'd thought about this moment for a long, long time, ever since she'd returned to Silver Springs. She'd imagined the moment she would come face-to-face with her first infatuation, a man who, as history had proved, would only see her as his older brother's high-school friend.

She hadn't imagined that she would be holding twenty-some pounds of wiggling trouble in her arms, that her dress would be streaked with sauce, that her hair and face would be as sticky as a mischievous little girl's hands.

Chagrined, she stiffly said, "It *has* been a while." More than a dozen years. "Obviously, there was nothing here for you before."

Reed's smile evaporated and Alcina realized he might have taken her wrong. She'd meant herself— that he wouldn't have come back because of her. Instead, she feared, her words had come out sounding like a criticism of his motives, his father being near death's door and all.

Reed set his hat back in place. "I think I'd better tend to my family…and let you tend to yours."

"Family?" she echoed, even as Hope wrenched around in her arms and squealed to be let down. "You mean Hope…oh, no, she's not mine. This is your brother's child, Reed. Chance and Pru's. She's your niece. Hope, honey, say hello to your uncle Reed."

Alcina couldn't help herself. The devil made her do it. She offered the sticky child to the middle Quarrels brother. Reed hesitated only a second before taking her. He certainly didn't seem squeamish about having a child in his arms, Alcina realized.

The two studied each other for a moment. Hope's expression became as intent as her uncle's, and Alcina was struck by a resemblance she hadn't expected to see.

And for a moment, her stomach fluttered as she imagined Reed holding his own child. *Their* child.

Nonsense!

She was a little old to have kids. At thirty-seven, her biological clock had almost run out of time. Besides, she had her status as the town spinster to uphold...even if the designation wasn't exactly accurate.

"So you're Hope," Reed said. "I've heard about you."

The little girl seemed as mesmerized by his smooth-whiskey voice as she was, Alcina thought. She clenched her jaw and told herself to stop salivating.

Reed Quarrels had never been attracted to her. He'd preferred spunky little tomboys who sat a horse well and knew all about beeves.

Suddenly shy, Hope turned her face away from Reed's and shrieked, "M'ma!"

"Mama's coming, sweetheart!"

Alcina noted that Pru and Chance were headed straight for them, other members of the Quarrels family following—Emmett, and Bart and his kids, Lainey and Daniel. A regular family reunion.

One to which she didn't belong.

Knowing when she wasn't needed, Alcina backed off unnoticed as Reed was surrounded. She headed for the house and a bathroom where she could clean up. Josie Walker, the Curly-Q wrangler and Bart's woman, was coming outside, carrying a big basket of corn bread.

Eyes widening, she asked, "What happened to you?"

"Hope."

"Ah-h." Josie nodded in understanding and looked past her. "So what's the big commotion? Is that who I think it is?"

"It's Reed."

"I'm so glad. Bart said he'd show."

Alcina didn't miss the inflection in Josie's voice at Bart's name—the woman was love struck. They would already be married if it weren't for his kids, who were still getting over their mother's tragic death the year before. Alcina admired the couple's patience. Josie and Bart were doing the right thing, giving the kids time to get used to the relationship.

Josie gave her a pointed look. "So, Reed's back— why are you hightailing it in the opposite direction?"

Pru had a big mouth, Alcina thought. It was one thing when her best friend teased *her* about her schoolgirl infatuation. Another when she got other people into the act...though to be fair, Josie was the only one Pru had told. As far as Alcina knew, anyway.

"I said hello," Alcina said, voice stiff.

"Uh-oh. Doesn't sound like it went well."

"With Reed, it never does."

"We'll have to work on that."

"Josie, don't try to play matchmaker," Alcina pleaded. "And if Pru comes up with any bright ideas about getting Reed and me together, I would appreciate your discouraging her."

"Oh, come on—"

"I'm serious. You have enough on your plate to take care of, anyway," Alcina said.

Things were working out so well between Josie and Bart's kids that Alcina figured it wouldn't be much longer before the couple made their relationship official.

"Let me give you some advice," Josie said. "Real love doesn't come around that often. And neither does a good man, as I very well know. So if you want Reed and you get a shot at him, take it. If you don't, you'll always wonder what might have been."

Josie had a point when it came to the *good man* part. But, as to her getting a shot at Reed…

The man barely knew she existed.

REUNITED WITH HIS FAMILY, Reed kept taking in Pa with disbelief. Emmett Quarrels was smaller than Reed remembered—they were about the same height now—and he'd lost weight in the past year. The shock of white hair and faded blue eyes were nothing new, but the sunken cheeks and sagging skin were, and they made him look older than his seventy years.

"I knew you wouldn't let me down, Son." Pa's declaration was followed by a dry cough that set Reed on edge.

"Hey, I thought this was my wedding," Chance complained.

"Don't be getting on your high horse here, Boy," Pa said. "You know what I mean."

If Chance was angry, he wasn't showing it. He and Pru were beaming in their happiness.

"I meant to be at the church," Reed told them both apologetically. "I really did. But there was something I had to take care of at the last minute on the Evergreen, so I started off late, and then I ran into a problem on the road."

"You're here now, Reed," Pru said. "That's all that counts, right, sweetheart?"

Chance flashed his teeth in a sincere-looking smile. "You bet, darlin', that's good enough for me."

The brothers threw their arms around each other in a manly hug. Reed was relieved that Chance accepted his regrets without questioning him about his actual situation.

"Congratulations, Chance. Do I get to kiss the bride now?"

"Only if you keep it short and sweet."

"Pru, welcome to the family," Reed said, hugging her and giving her a quick kiss. *"Finally."*

Which was all he would say on the matter. Considering their daughter was nearly two years old, it was about time his brother made an honest woman of Pru.

"Good to see you, Reed," Bart said, slapping him on the back. "And it'll be good working together again."

Together? Or would he be working for Bart?

Another thing that ate at Reed, though he kept that to himself, as well.

A few minutes of catch-up and his niece Lainey was agitating for photographs of the three brothers together.

"Better be careful," Reed's sixteen-year-old nephew Daniel warned them. "Lainey thinks she's an artist. She might make you do some weird stuff."

"You're the weirdo," Lainey told her brother.

Reed grinned. The siblings reminded him of Chance and Bart when they'd been kids.

As Lainey painstakingly photographed them in several different poses, Reed's attention wandered a bit. He kept musing on Alcina's whereabouts.

Always the proper lady with every hair in place,

she'd shown him a new side of herself today. A side
that had intrigued him. He'd remembered her as being
prissy—actually, she'd gotten a little prissy earlier
when he'd laughed at her. She'd been so natural with
Hope, though, not worrying about her own finery.
Seeing her like that had roused his curiosity.

"Uncle Reed, you're not paying attention!" Lainey
complained. "You've got to smile."

Reed did his best to please her.

One more photograph and Chance said, "Okay,
that's it for now, Lainey. We'd best get to the grub
quick, before all those old bachelor cowboys who are
normally deprived of good home-cooking get in line
for seconds. Then we'll starve to death."

Having noted the huge quantity of food laid out,
Reed thought that was a gross exaggeration. And,
even though the brothers were the last to reach the
buffet table, none of them would go hungry.

Undoubtedly Chance was anxious to get back to
his new bride and daughter, and Reed could hardly
blame him.

He admitted to a bit of healthy jealousy as he
watched Chance rejoin Pru and kiss her as if they'd
been apart for years instead of mere minutes. Somehow that kind of love had never come his way. Working six or seven days a week as he usually did, Reed
doubted that he would ever have time to look for it,
either. Maybe he was destined to be another old bachelor cowboy.

The band started up as he filled his plate with Felice's finest. Reed dipped his head in time to the music. He looked over to the dance floor as Pru and
Chance stepped up, followed by two other couples.

So much for his brother's appetite, Reed thought, grinning to himself.

His plate in hand, Reed was leaving the buffet, when he felt as if he was being watched. The short hairs at the back of his neck shot to attention. Warily, he turned to meet the gaze of a burly man with pale eyes and a white buzz cut. Then Reed realized the man was standing behind the makeshift bar. It was only the bartender, for pity's sake.

The man waved him over with one hand, lifted an empty glass with the other.

Feeling foolish, Reed complied.

"You must be brother number three. Hugh Ruskin—I tend bar over at the Silver Slipper."

Ruskin held out a hand heavy with expensive rings that Reed wouldn't expect to see on a bartender. He gave the man a quick shake.

"Reed Quarrels. That old saloon is still going, huh?"

"A man's got to have a place to quench his thirst, even in a small town like Silver Springs," Ruskin said. "So what's your pleasure?"

"Whatever's on tap will do."

Ruskin filled a mug. "I hear you've been working up in Colorado, running the show on some spread ten times the size of this one."

"For the past few years," Reed agreed, wondering why he should be the focus of town gossip. "Though someone exaggerated the size of the Evergreen."

"Still, when you're used to running a major operation like that one…"

Ruskin was peering at him closely as if waiting for him to spill his guts. Say how unhappy he was to be back or something. Reed figured the bartender got some kick out of keeping his finger on the pulse of the town, having juicy tidbits to spread around to his patrons.

Could the man really know about his hesitancy at returning? About the problematic dynamics between him and Bart? Or was he just fishing?

Not about to fuel any gossip, Reed picked up his mug and sipped the head off the beer. "You know what they say…nothing like home."

Something flashed through the other man's pale eyes. Something that unsettled Reed.

And the bartender's thumbs-up sign and his "Gotcha there, my friend," seemed a little forced.

Wondering about Hugh Ruskin—where he came from, what he was doing tending bar in a backwater town like Silver Springs—Reed saluted him with the beer and left the bar. Uneasy still, he made a mental note to ask Bart or Chance about the bartender later.

In the meantime, he quickly scanned the crowd until he spotted Alcina, who was sitting at the end of a table under a couple of big cottonwoods. Her long fingers with perfectly manicured nails were worrying the stem of a wineglass as if she was distracted. The plate before her was half-empty and pushed far enough in front of her to indicate she'd finished eating.

Her golden-blond hair was pulled up into a French twist, but fine wisps curled at her temples and down her long, elegant neck, which was circled by a single strand of pearls. He'd bet they were real, too. Her finely cut profile was free of the barbecue sauce that had decorated it earlier. A lovely woman, indeed, Reed thought appreciatively, not having seen her the last time he'd come home for a visit. The seat next to her was vacant.

He hesitated, mulled over the advisability of the notion that struck him, and in the end, headed for her table.

Listening to Reba Gantry, the flamboyant owner of Reba's Café, who was waving around a half-empty whiskey glass—she could drink nearly as much as a man and often did—Alcina didn't even notice his approach until he asked, "Mind if I join you?"

She started, her gray eyes widening on him for a moment. Recovering quickly, she indicated the empty chair. "It's your spread."

"Only by default." He set down his plate and mug and slid into the vacant seat, where he got a better look at her finery. "You cleaned up real nice, but it looks like Hope ruined your party dress for good."

She shrugged. "It's not the end of the world."

"Some women would think so."

"Good thing I'm not some women."

Good thing, Reed agreed, digging into Felice's homemade enchilada, Alcina interesting him even more than before. He realized how little he knew about her even though they'd grown up in the same town. Then, he hadn't been interested in an older woman—to a teenage boy, three years difference in age had been a whole generation. Now three years was nothing.

"We missed you at the church," Reba said, taking a swig of whiskey and holding it in her mouth for a moment.

"Something came up," he said vaguely, swallowing a mouthful of *posole.* "Mighty fine duds there."

He admired the café owner's ability to pull off

wearing such an eye-popping rose-trimmed purple dress. Then, as he remembered, Reba had always had a natural flair for the dramatic.

"You're looking fine yourself, honey," Reba said. "It's real good to see you again." She indicated the big man who sat next to her. "I'd like to introduce you to my dear friend, Cesar Cardona."

"Howdy," Reed said.

Cardona looked to be in his late forties, a quantity of silver lightening his thick dark hair and full mustache. Wearing a black suit, the short jacket trimmed with silver braid and silver and turquoise conchos, he was definitely Reba's male counterpart, Reed thought with amusement.

But Reed's enjoyment faded when the café owner said, "Cesar is bringing new life and jobs to the area around Silver Springs. He's a land developer—"

"Let me guess," Reed cut in, giving the newcomer a piercing stare. "Land of Enchantment Acres."

Cardona's teeth flashed white against his sun-warmed skin. "So you've heard of us." The meatiness of the hand he reached across the table was softened by a heavily jeweled watchband.

Taking it, though reluctantly, Reed realized the raw power of the big man. "Saw the sign driving in. I can hardly believe Gonzalez sold. His family owned that land for nearly two hundred years."

"That land kept Luis Gonzalez poor."

"I guess it depends on your definition of poor," Reed argued. "Being land-rich in God's country in this part of New Mexico goes a long way to making up for the things a man can't afford to buy himself."

Cardona shrugged and spread his hands. "Well, now Luis can buy whatever he wants."

"I wonder what that might be," Reed muttered, stabbing his fork into the mashed potatoes.

While Gonzalez's spread had been small—little more than four thousand acres—ranching was the only life the man had ever known and he was barely fifty. What would he do with his days for the next twenty years? Reed himself couldn't imagine working at anything but ranching, which occupied his whole being. When he got busy, he might not even get into town for weeks and never once miss it.

As if she sensed his rising tension over the matter, Alcina veered the discussion in a slightly different direction. "Are the new properties selling well, Cesar?"

"Like hotcakes," the developer said, grinning. 'I can't get the houses built fast enough."

Suddenly losing his appetite, Reed asked, "So we're in for how many new people in the area?"

"I sold off nearly half the acreage to the VM Ranch, so there'll only be about twenty new families—people who have always wanted a real piece of the West for themselves. I'm not raping the land if that's what you're worried about. I'm keeping properties at a minimum of a hundred acres."

"Sounds sensible," Alcina said. "And good for Silver Springs."

Gut tightening, Reed didn't say anything.

Luis Gonzalez would never have sold an acre to Vernon Martell, a virtual newcomer to Silver Springs. The Hispanic ranchers in the area were tight-knit and didn't sell their land to Anglos. Martell had gotten around that through Cardona, whose only loyalty obviously was to the almighty dollar.

"Actually, I'm already looking around for another spread," Cardona went on. "Got to plan ahead."

Reed didn't like the way the man was looking around at the Curly-Q, as if he was already viewing it as a commodity and planning on subdividing it next.

"The Curly-Q's not for sale," he said quietly but firmly. "So don't go getting any ideas about this place."

Reed was dead serious, but Cardona laughed.

"Everything's for sale, my friend. You merely gotta figure out the right incentive to get what you want."

As far as Reed was concerned, that ended the conversation.

Reba put a beringed hand on her escort's shoulder. "Cesar, honey, I sure am in the mood for a dance."

Cardona immediately got to his feet and helped her out of her chair. "I'd never say no to holding you in my arms."

Reba swayed a little as if the drinking had caught up to her. Then she shook herself straight and headed for the dance floor.

They'd barely left the table when Alcina spoke up, her tone indignant. "I'm surprised at you, Reed Quarrels. You never used to be so rude!"

Chapter Two

Startled, Reed stared at Alcina. "What's rude about speaking my mind?"

It was something he usually avoided. He didn't know what had gotten into him.

Yes, he did, Reed admitted.

Truth be told, his whole way of life was being threatened by men like Cardona. Ranches all over the West were being sold off and carved up into smaller properties. Peoples' lifelong dreams were being stolen away from them, and with the economy so poor for those that lived off the land, there didn't seem to be a way to stop it.

A man practically had to have another job to support his ranch habit. Or his wife did.

"The area needs new blood," Alcina said, "or Silver Springs will die."

"It *is* dead. Has been for years. It's a ghost town, but certain people don't want to let it go."

"Which includes your father," she reminded him. "Emmett wants to see it come back. So do I."

So did he, for that matter, not that he would admit it now.

"I heard you opened yourself a business," he said,

instead, "inviting people who don't belong here to come this way."

"You mean tourists?" she asked, a sudden chill in her tone. "What's wrong with letting people from other parts of the country see how beautiful this area is…and my making a living off their interest."

"Because then they get too interested and want to move right in on our territory."

"Well, good for them. And good for us. Time doesn't stand still, Reed, no matter how much you might want it to. Things change. Businesses change. People change—"

"Including you?"

"What do you mean by that?"

"Just that I'm surprised you came back to Silver Springs at all," Reed admitted. "Why did you? I figured you fit right in on the East Coast with your mother's people."

Emotions washed through her face so quickly he imagined he might have upset her.

"Are you saying I don't fit in here?" she demanded.

"Do you?"

"Not everyone has to be a rancher or a rancher's wife to love the high-desert country. Silver Springs used to rely on the silver mine, but it dried up years ago and so did the town. And so did anything resembling a life for me here."

Alcina was working up a head of steam as she spoke. Reed couldn't help but be mesmerized by her heightened color and the way her features so quickly became animated, making her appear even more beautiful.

"But there is hope, Reed," she went on hotly,

''and that hope is new blood and new ideas. So what if my way of being able to live here meant turning our old home into a bed-and-breakfast? It was that or drive into Taos or some other town that's at least solvent to make a living. Then I would be commuting again and...oh, never mind.''

Alcina shoved herself from the table and rose. Reed hadn't meant to insult her into leaving, but he figured she was through listening, for the moment, anyway. Besides, he'd said too much as it was. Normally, he kept his nose out of other people's business and his opinions to himself where they belonged.

If he had, she might not be stalking away from him in disgust, her patrician nose in the air.

More than anything, Reed craved peace in his life, no doubt a reaction to his fractious childhood. He'd grown up in a household where his father and two brothers had constantly warred with each other. Reed had vowed he never would live like that again.

So why was he finding the outspoken woman so attractive? Reed wondered.

He forced himself to remain seated rather than follow her. He could use a woman in his life, true, but he could do without Alcina Dale.

Disgusted at how his supper conversation had turned sour, Reed tried to muster his appetite in vain. Half of the food he'd piled on his plate would be wasted.

Then he remembered the dog.

After throwing away the bones and scraping away some of the spicier stuff, he was satisfied that the leftovers would do. He found an empty bowl, filled it with water, then headed back toward his truck.

On the way, he spotted Pa near the house, deep in

conversation with Vernon Martell, whom he'd met on his last visit home. The man was alone, his wife being an invalid who rarely got out. Reed meant to say howdy.

The neighboring rancher was a hearty man, tall and broad-shouldered, not trim, but not heart-attack material, either. In his mid-forties, he wore his light brown hair short, and his equally light brown eyes peered through fashionable titanium-framed bifocals. He was plain dressed—at least compared to Cardona—but he appeared equally well-heeled from the looks of his custom boots, chamois sports coat and heavy diamond-studded gold cuff links that said a lot about his healthy bank account.

Drawing closer, he heard Martell say, "I'm in the market to expand the VM."

"You already did with that land you got from that developer fella."

The tone of the conversation stopped Reed in his tracks.

Vernon Martell was new to the area, so to speak, having lived in these parts little more than a year. Denizens of the community were considered in terms of generations, or at least decades, rather than in months or years. Besides which, Martell had picked up a ranch that had folded under economic stress dirt cheap—a foreclosure—and that didn't win any popularity contests. Neither would his buying a chunk of Luis Gonzalez's land.

"That was a start," Martell agreed, "but I'm not finished."

Instinct made Reed stay where he was, a few yards behind the men. Wanting to hear what they had to say, he chose not to interrupt.

"You must've had a better year than the Curly-Q." Emmett Quarrels narrowed his gaze on his neighbor. "What did you have in mind?"

"Your southernmost pastures—they adjoin the land that belonged to Gonzalez."

"So what's your point?"

"That we could both come out ahead," Martell said magnanimously. "Me with a little more land, you with enough money so that you don't lose the rest."

"I'm not losin' nothing."

"That's not the word going around. Word is that Tucker Dale is ready to foreclose—"

"Gossip is fodder for old women with nothing better to do!" Emmett snapped, cutting him off.

Reed could hardly believe it. Tucker Dale, Alcina's father and Pa's longtime former business partner, threatening Pa with ruin.

Martell persisted. "So the rumors aren't true?"

"It's none of your business. Unless…you wouldn't know anything about the bad-luck incidents plaguing the Curly-Q lately?"

"Are you accusing me of something?"

Pa seemed to be mulling that over, Reed realized, after which he choked out, "All I'm saying is that I expect you should mind your own spread and keep your nose out of mine!"

With that, Pa stomped off. Martell stared after him for a moment before turning and coming face-to-face with Reed. Their gazes locked. The other rancher was the first to look away. He waved to some invisible acquaintance and stalked off in the other direction.

Leaving Reed uneasier than ever. He'd known the

Curly-Q was in trouble from his talk with Bart. But the seriousness of the situation suddenly hit him hard.

His gut told him that he'd walked back into a worse hornet's nest than he'd left more than a decade ago.

"EVERYTHING IS SET for your honeymoon night," Alcina told Pru when they met directly outside the ranch house, where she'd gone to regroup after her cross words with Reed.

"This is so great of you, so special." Pru pushed the red curls from her freckled face, gave Alcina a big hug.

"Special for a special friend," Alcina said.

She'd decked out the best suite at her bed-and-breakfast—the Springs—with dozens of candles, special scented bubble bath for the Jacuzzi and rose petals strewn across the spread. She'd also left a bottle of champagne set in a big bucket of ice next to the bed. Hopefully, it would still be cold when the newlyweds arrived—a lot of hours had passed, and it was already dusk.

"The spare key is in the cactus pot to the right of the front door," she reminded Pru. "Don't let Chance get bit," she joked as if she meant the cactus, "unless you do the biting, of course."

Laughing, Pru said, "A little privacy right now sounds like the best wedding present in the world."

Newlyweds living with the bride's family until other arrangements could be made wouldn't be easy on any of them, Alcina knew, and they were saving their honeymoon for the National Rodeo Finals to be held in Las Vegas, Nevada, in two weeks. She was happy to do this for Pru and Chance. She only wished she could let them have the bed-and-breakfast to themselves all night, but there was no place in town for her to bunk in, and Josie couldn't really stay with Bart because of his kids. At least no other guests were checked in—not that Alcina couldn't use more business.

"You'll have several hours alone, anyway, so you can get as wild as you want," Alcina teased. "Josie and I will give you fair warning when we come in— we'll make lots of noise."

Pru's eyebrows arched as she said, "Maybe if you're lucky, that'll be really, really late."

"How late do you want me to be?"

"As late as a certain Quarrels brother will keep you happily occupied."

Knowing what Pru was getting at, Alcina felt her grin fade. "You're dreaming." Thinking of the argument she'd had with Reed earlier, she said, "I'm the last woman Reed Quarrels would want to keep out late."

"I don't know. He was looking pretty interested."

"*Was* being the operative word. And then I opened my big mouth." Alcina sighed and wondered if she should have listened to his opinions and held her own, something she'd never gotten used to doing. "No man likes to hear a woman rant while he's held captive like a pinned butterfly."

"Hmm, sounds pretty darn interesting if you ask me." Coming up from behind them, Chance slipped an arm around his new wife's waist. "Making exotic plans for the evening, are you, Miss Prudence?"

Pru blushed and smacked him in the chest with the flat of her hand.

"Want to play rough, huh?" He grinned and arched one eyebrow. "How about we—"

"Enough already!" Alcina said with a laugh. "Too much information. I don't need any more details. And I think the two of you had better get out of here so you can be alone before you embarrass everyone."

Chance grinned. "Sounds like a plan."

"Not until we observe the formalities," Pru countered.

The formalities being the cake cutting and garter and bouquet throws, Alcina knew.

But first Pru wanted to freshen up. And Chance followed her inside the house, meaning the *formalities* wouldn't commence for some time yet.

Alcina started off, intending on rejoining the party, when she realized that she'd be on the sidelines watching couples dance. Forget that, she chose to take herself for some solitary exercise instead.

With dusk came a chill in the high-desert air. Alcina wrapped the scrap of material that matched her dress around her shoulders closer. Good thing she'd fetched it while in the house.

As she strolled behind the storage building that also held the living quarters of the only permanent hand on the Curly-Q, a loud thump startled her.

"Moon-Eye?" she called out.

But if the hired hand was around, he must not have heard, because he didn't answer.

On edge, she rounded the storage building and looked for the hired hand. Deep shadows thrust across the property, so it was difficult to make out details at any distance. Still, a movement from the back of the barn caught her attention. Of course it must be Moon-Eye—who else?—though she couldn't actually see the man well enough to be certain.

Alcina guessed chores on a ranch didn't wait, not

even for a wedding. She thought to join the hired hand, to keep him company for a few minutes, when a voice coming from the opposite direction distracted her.

"C'mon...I know you want it..."

A man's enticing voice.

"That's it, sweetheart..."

Reed's voice.

"That's good, isn't it?"

Alcina's mouth went dry at the seductive tone.

"I told you it would be..."

Who in the world was out here with him? Alcina wondered, her imagination on overdrive. Like a fool, she found herself wanting the full picture.

"More, yes...take it all..."

Shocked by the implication and yet drawn like a moth to a flame, she came close enough to see for herself.

And then her face flamed with her foolishness.

For, hunkered down next to his truck, Reed was hand-feeding a wretched-looking brown and white dog with a torn ear. The moment the animal spotted her, it backed off toward the pickup, cowering.

"You scared her," Reed stated. "Damn! And I was just getting her to come around."

Alcina ignored the blame placed on her and murmured, "Oh, no, girl, you don't need to be afraid of me," crouching also and holding out a nonthreatening hand.

Aware of Reed staring at her, Alcina grew self-conscious, but she didn't want to scare the dog further and so stayed exactly as she was. Barely a moment went by before the animal ventured forward to smell her fingers.

"You poor thing," Alcina said, turning her hand so the dog lightly nuzzled her palm. In the same tone, she asked Reed, "Where did she come from?"

"Not here. I found her on the road—the reason I was late. I'd never ask you to lie, but if you wouldn't tell Chance…"

She remembered him being honest to a fault, so his keeping something like that from his brother was a big deal. *Reed confiding in her…* Warmth flooded Alcina.

"I think Chance would understand, but I'll keep mum."

She'd always known Reed was a kind man. Without thinking, she stroked the dog's neck, then continued petting her, running a hand down a bony spine.

Suddenly catching herself, Alcina murmured, "Oh, sorry."

She expected the dog to slither away and was surprised when it moved closer for more.

"She must trust you," Reed said.

Alcina ran gentle fingers along the animal's protruding ribs. "You don't have to sound so surprised."

"I didn't mean that to sound judgmental. It's just that she's so skittish."

Suddenly feeling a little skittish herself, Alcina met Reed's gaze and realized that he was staring at her. His expression was appreciative. And puzzling.

"What?" she asked.

He shrugged. "Most women wouldn't have touched a dog that looked scruffy and sick."

"I'm not—"

"Most women," he finished for her. "I remember."

Getting to her feet, Alcina asked, "So what's her name?"

"I don't know. She's not my dog."

A disbelieving Alcina cleared her throat.

"She's not." Reed rose, as well. "But I intend to find her a good home."

From the way the dog was looking at him so adoringly, Alcina figured she'd already found herself one—her new owner obviously hadn't realized it yet.

"In the meantime," she said, "you have to call her something."

"What's wrong with Girl?"

"Not very personal."

"Then what do you suggest?" he asked.

"You want me to name your...uh, her?"

"Why not? It's only temporary."

"Right, temporary." Alcina looked deep into the dog's liquid brown eyes. "Hey, Temporary."

The dog whistled through her nose and gave a sharp bark.

"I think she likes it," Alcina said.

Reed snorted. "Temporary? Come on, that's a ridiculous name for a dog."

"Then you name her."

For a moment, she thought Reed might take her challenge. Then he shrugged.

"Temporary it is."

Alcina grinned. They stood there grinning at each other for a moment before she remembered the festivities. She'd only meant to kill a few minutes and had lost track of time.

"I think we'd better get back if we want to send the bride and groom off with our best wishes," she said.

"That means it's time for you to get back into the pickup," Reed told the dog.

He patted her and opened the door. She stood there looking at him.

Giving her a hand signal, he said, "C'mon, Temporary, get in."

The dog jumped into the truck and onto the driver's seat where she settled, her adoring gaze still on Reed.

"You're her hero," Alcina murmured.

"I only did what any decent person would do."

She knew that wasn't true. The world was filled with *decent* folks. But the dog obviously had been on her own for a while now. Only a really caring person would have taken the time and trouble with her that Reed had.

With the dog settled, they hurried back to the party to find the wedding cake had already been cut, and the unmarried men were being urged to step up for the garter toss.

Nearly two dozen men, mostly old bachelor cowboys, got into the spirit of the competition. Moon-Eye was at the front of the line, she noted; he must have finished his chores. Even Bart and Reed jostled each other good-naturedly as one of the musicians beat a tattoo on his drum.

Chance took a quick look over his shoulder, and Alcina was certain he aimed directly for Bart, who was committed, if not yet officially engaged, to Josie Walker.

Only, Reed was the one who ended up with the garter on his arm.

Alcina tried to sit out the bouquet throw, but Pru wouldn't hear of it. Certain her friend would send the spray of flowers Josie's way, Alcina gave in and moved to the opposite side of the much smaller group of women, the oldest of whom was Felice, the youngest Lainey.

When the bouquet wound up in her own hands, Alcina was floored.

Pru turned to face her, a sly grin quirking her lips, and Alcina knew her friend had sent the flowers her way purposely. What in the world was she thinking?

Just then, the band started a lively tune.

"Well, isn't this an interesting development," Pru said, drawing closer, Chance in tow. She shifted her mischievous gaze from Alcina to Reed.

"You *really* shouldn't have," Alcina muttered.

A challenging glitter in his eyes, Reed asked, "Alcina Dale, where's your spirit of fun?"

And before Alcina knew what was happening, he'd swung her into his arms for a dance.

As they did the Texas two-step, the newlyweds grabbed hands and rushed through the dancing crowd. Catcalls about their wedding night and handfuls of birdseed followed them. Alcina watched them go with a bit of envy, the emotion exacerbated, no doubt, by the man who wrapped his arms around her.

"Amazing, Chance settling down," Reed said. "I never thought I'd see the day."

"People do strange things when the love bug bites them."

Alcina was only too aware of something nibbling at her.

After the disagreement that had punctuated their reunion, who would have thought she would end up in Reed's arms? Being there felt too good for her peace of mind, Alcina decided. He was merely getting into the spirit of the occasion, while she was feeling things that made her chafe.

She wasn't a teenager anymore...not even a young woman...so what was her problem?

While she'd thought of Reed fondly through the years, she hadn't kept herself on a shelf waiting for him to realize that she was *the one* for him. She'd gone on with her life, tc other men, other relationships. She'd returned to New Mexico after college in New York, but she'd soon had reason to return to the East Coast. Working as an interior designer, she'd met plenty of eligible New York bachelors. Her friends out East had considered her sophisticated when it came to matters of the heart after her seemingly easy split with Jeffrey.

But suddenly she was thrust back to the uncertainty of her youth. Sweaty palms. Palpitating heart. Overactive imagination.

Surely it was only her sentimental streak at work. That and a healthy libido.

The moment the music ended, Alcina thought to put a stop to her renewed attraction to Reed right then and there, but the band merely swung into a softer, easier piece, and he pulled her even closer. They fit together perfectly, his chin resting against her temple. His warm breath drifted across her forehead and shot goose bumps down her spine.

Alcina groaned.

"Am I holding you too tight?"

"No...yes."

"Make up your mind. Which is it?"

Alcina made a big show of adjusting the bouquet that lay along his back. She murmured, "There, that's better,'' as if holding the flowers had been her problem.

"Mmm."

She wasn't about to let him know that *he* was the cause of her discomfort. But now his breath was tickling her ear. A tiny thrill traveled all the way down to her toes. She tightened her hold on the bouquet, and the fingers of her other hand pressed into the garter.

The significance of the wedding tokens didn't escape her.

Despite her being a rational, sensible, self-reliant woman, she wished—only for a moment—that old traditions had some basis in fact. That a bridal bouquet and a garter really were good-luck charms that could turn her youthful fantasies into adult reality.

Then Reed turned his head to gaze into her eyes, and his face slowly inched closer, and a little smile played across his lips, and crazily—only for a moment—she thought he was about to kiss her.

Pulse jagging, reality returning in a rush, Alcina ended that moment fast.

She stopped dead on the dance floor and pushed at Reed's chest until he released her. Staring at him, hardly able to catch her breath, she felt too foolish for words.

"Something wrong?" he asked, that knowing smile still flirting with his mouth.

"Something, yes…"

Like her heart pounding as fast as a freight train…
…and her knees softening to Jell-O…
…and her brain turning to mush.

"But don't worry about it, okay?" she gasped.

With that, Alcina rushed off the dance floor and cut through the noisy revelers.

"Alcina, wait a minute," Reed called.

Not stopping, she nevertheless glanced over her shoulder and saw him still standing on the dance floor, hands on his hips and staring after her as if she were a crazy person. So much for any attraction that had sparked between them, she thought. After this, added to their earlier fight, he'd be sure to keep his distance.

Chagrined, she fled toward the buildings and the refuge of her car that was parked on the other side. Not that she could go home, she realized—she'd promised Pru some quality time with her new husband.

She was thinking that she'd go for a long drive and was trying to visualize where, when a series of weird noises cut through her jumbled thoughts.

A muffled boom was followed by a high-pitched outcry...several horses, she realized...horrible noises tearing from their throats.

Equine screams that sent gooseflesh down her spine.

The music died abruptly and voices rose behind her as she ducked between buildings. Drawn to the disturbance on the other side, she gasped in shock and fear, and for a moment stopped, frozen at the sight.

The barn was ablaze and three horses milled about before it. The animals were trapped in the small corral adjacent to the burning building.

"Dear Lord!"

The blaze was growing, and as sparks shot into the dry brush surrounding the fence, the lines of fire spread so fast that Alcina could hardly take in the reality of what she was witnessing. Inside the corral, the screaming horses—three of them—stood out in dark silhouette against the orange glow. One of them reared, frantic hooves slashing at the pipe and wire fencing.

The gate!

Dropping the bouquet, Alcina ran for all she was worth as another explosion shot the flames higher and wider. If the horses weren't freed fast, they would either burn to death or injure themselves, perhaps fatally, while trying to escape.

Unlatching the gate, she swung it open wide. Immediately one horse popped out as if greased and goosed.

Alcina whistled and shouted, "C'mon!" to the others. She stood back to give them a wide berth.

A second horse shot past her.

But a third continued to screech and dance in circles, seemingly too terrified to recognize the safety of the opening. And another whistle from Alcina didn't seem to cut through his panic.

A roar of voices behind her told Alcina that help was on its way. Someone else who knew more about horses would have a better chance of rescuing the creature. A glance over her shoulder assured her that she was the only one close enough to help now before it was too late.

Heart pounding, she ducked through the opening. Someone cried, "Alcina, stop!" but she was too focused on the terrified horse to heed the warning.

"Easy," she crooned. "I'm going to get you out of here. You'll be all right."

The horse snorted, threw up his head and rolled his eyes at her in distrust. He wasn't going to come easily, that was for certain. Maybe if she got around behind him, she could drive him out.

As Alcina drew closer, the terrified horse acted cornered. Screaming, the bay reared, then bolted forward as if ready to drive right through her. Alcina tried her best to get out of his way, but she wasn't fast enough.

Half a ton of panicked horse glanced off her shoulder. Alcina flew back, stars of pain and orange flames and flailing yellow silk filling her vision for the few seconds she was airborne. Then she landed hard, all the breath knocked out of her.

She couldn't move.

The fire raged closer...its greedy heat licked her.

Stunned, she watched a spark land on the tip of her silk wrap.

Like a fuse, it ignited.

Chapter Three

"Alcina!" Reed cried again as the bay shot through the opening, scattering a handful of men who'd converged around the perimeter of the fire.

Fire...

Her shawl...

And Alcina wasn't moving!

Fear squeezed his gut as Reed ducked into the corral even as she untangled herself from the material and rolled away from the new burst of flames. Mere seconds later, Reed was at her side, stomping on the burning silk. Voices rose behind him—Pa and Bart shouting orders to control the fire before it spread to the storage shed or bunkhouse.

Alcina was struggling to sit. Doused in the orange glow of the reflected flames, she appeared strangely calm.

"I've got you," he muttered, swooping down and pulling her to her feet. "Can you walk?"

She choked out, "I think so," but Reed realized she was having trouble breathing.

Cursing, he lifted her into his arms and carried her out of what had grown into a nearly complete ring of flames.

Men and women in their Sunday best had pitched in to fight the fire. A bucket brigade formed from a nearby horse trough and a stream of water from the garden hose hit the flames. People scraped an area ahead of the fire bare so it had nothing to feed on, while others shoveled loose soil over burning grasses or used wet burlap feed sacks to beat back the smaller flames.

And Bart seemed to be everywhere at once. In charge. In control. As usual.

But Bart's being in the saddle was after the fact. He hadn't been able to stop that fire from starting. Certain that he'd heard something weird, Reed was wondering exactly what had happened, when he noticed one of the guests leaving alone.

Vernon Martell.

Reed guessed the newcomer didn't want to get his fancy leather jacket or new boots messed up.

Alcina pushed at his chest. "Reed, you can let me down."

"If I did, I would probably just have to pick you up again." His temper flared. "All that dry brush catching fire, whatever possessed you to go into that corral, woman?"

"That's Alcina to you," she said icily. "My being a woman has nothing to do with it. I was merely trying to save one of your precious horses from being added to Felice's platters of barbecue."

Reed figured Alcina hadn't intended to be funny, but the black humor of her comment got to him, and he couldn't help himself. He snorted. He couldn't stop, either. Not all the way to the ranch house, where he carried her straight inside. The whole time, she lay in his arms, stiff as a cord of wood. Her lips didn't even twitch once that he could see.

Reaching the deserted kitchen, he set her down and was relieved that she was steady on her feet. He probably could leave her alone in good conscience. After all, everyone was outside fighting the fire.

Everyone but the two of them.

Torn between a sense of duty and pity for the woman who had taken him away from it, Reed took a good long look at his older brother's childhood friend, the daughter of their pa's former partner and current enemy.

Grime streaked her dress and dappled her creamy skin. He skittered his gaze away from the top of her bodice where ash marbled her breasts, and let his eyes wander up her long, elegant, black-striped neck. Her hair was soot-laden, as well, and dirty strands tumbled from their pins. A regular bird's nest, only not so neat.

"You're a mess," he stated flatly.

"You don't look so great yourself," Alcina grumbled.

Reed rubbed a smudge from her chin and then held it steady so he could gaze deeply into her eyes.

He was looking for a concussion...

What he got was caught.

He didn't quite know how it happened, but when Alcina's gray eyes went all wide and soft on him, Reed felt his mouth go dry and his gut knot.

"I—I really am all right," she said. "Thanks to you. I do thank you for rescuing me."

Alcina sounded oddly breathless.

Reed felt a little short-winded himself.

Still, he said, "Knowing you, you would have rescued yourself, given another minute or two." He found himself smoothing a thumb over her grimy cheek. "But I'm glad I could be of service." A little soot couldn't hide her sheer beauty and Reed wondered why her looks had never impressed him before. "Dollars to doughnuts you really are all right, but I think you should see Doc—"

"No. Really. I'll probably be bruised and stiff in the morning, but nothing's broken," she insisted. "He'll merely tell me what I already know to do, sensible things like take a couple of aspirin, get in a hot shower and then apply an ice pack to the sore spots."

She'd always been that beautiful, Reed guessed...but had she always been so stubborn?

He said, "If you won't agree to see the doctor, maybe I ought to inspect those sore spots myself."

Not that he normally worked on people; he usually kept his doctoring skills to ranch animals.

"I don't think so." Alcina's gaze narrowed on him and she crossed her arms over her chest. "Our relationship isn't that personal."

Getting her drift, he muttered, "Oh."

"Yes, oh!" she said with extra emphasis.

Which made him want to check all the more.

He was having a moment of clarity, Reed realized. Normally ambivalent about the women who passed through his life, he was more interested in Miss Alcina Dale than he should be, considering the way her daddy and his pa had been fighting mad at each other for years.

She shifted uncomfortably under his close gaze. "So maybe you'd better get back outside."

"Right." He backed off a bit, but suspicions were

niggling at him. "Before I go, answer me something, would you?"

"If I can."

"You beat everyone else to the barn." He didn't want to think the fire was anything but an accident, but after the cryptic hints about this and that going wrong on the spread that he'd gotten from Bart, he had to assume the worst. "You didn't see anything unusual, right?"

"Other than the fire? No. But maybe you ought to ask Moon-Eye."

"Why Moon-Eye?"

"He was out there earlier."

"In the barn? When?"

"I saw him right before I spotted you with the dog," Alcina said. "I mean, I really couldn't see who the man was for sure, but I assumed that it was Moon-Eye...doing chores."

Frowning, Reed shook his head. "As far as I know, Moon-Eye never left the party."

"Then if he wasn't in the barn..." Alcina's forehead creased. "Who was?"

Who, indeed?

THE CRISIS WAS OVER, Alcina realized when she left the house a few minutes after Reed. Thankfully, the fire had been extinguished. Some people were standing around talking, while others were already heading for their vehicles.

Obviously, the festivities were over, as well.

Reba Gantry and her escort stopped nearby, their voices low in a heated discussion. The café owner's finery had been ruined, but somehow Cesar Cardona had managed to remain picture-perfect, as if the land developer had stood back to watch the barn burn.

Reba's voice suddenly rose, carrying across the few yards that separated them from Alcina. "I wouldn't keep anything this valuable without trying to find the rightful owner!"

"It wouldn't be like you stole anything!" Cardona growled. "Think of it as payment for the clothes you ruined doing your good deed. A reward."

Puzzled, Alcina took a better look at the couple and noted something sparkly in the café owner's hand.

Cardona continued to argue. "Anyone could have lost it. You'll never find the person."

"Not if I don't ask around, I won't."

"Even if you do, how do you know whoever claims it is the rightful owner? What if I told you that *I* lost it?"

"I'd call you a damn liar and then some, Cesar Cardona. You don't fool me none. I know the kinds of things you've been up to around here." Appearing as disgusted as she sounded, Reba glanced around and, when she saw Alcina, headed her way, waving the sparkly object that was the focus of the couple's argument. "Say, honey, you didn't lose a diamond tonight, did you?"

Alcina shook her head. "I prefer pearls."

"What about Pru? Could this have come from her engagement ring?"

Alcina took a closer look at the trillion—a triangular-shaped unmounted diamond.

"Nope. Wrong cut." And unusual. "Where did you find it?"

Reba pointed. "Over by the entrance to the barn. Rather, what's left of it. I was swatting down some flames with wet burlap when this beauty nearly jumped up and bit me.''

Staring down at the sparkling diamond in her dirty hand, Reba wore a wistful look. No doubt she would like the gem for herself, Alcina thought, admiring her honest nature.

She suggested, ''It probably belongs to one of the other women who were fighting the fire in the same area.''

''Nope, already asked them.'' Reba sighed and pocketed the stone. ''But the diamond belongs to someone, so I'd better get a move on and spread the word that I have it before the party breaks up.''

The party had broken up with the first whiff of smoke, but Alcina didn't bother clarifying.

''Cesar?'' Reba called, making a one-eighty. ''Now, where did that man go?''

Alcina spotted him climbing into his shiny black truck. ''Uh-oh, looks like he lost patience with you. If you need a ride back to town, let me know.''

Following Alcina's gaze, Reba muttered, ''Well, I never...! He'd better not come back sniffing around me for what he's not welcome to anymore, that's all I have to say.''

With that, the café owner marched off and approached a small knot of people standing near the parked cars.

Alcina wasn't aware of Hugh Ruskin until he said, ''That was a real brave thing you did, ma'am, putting yourself in the thick of the fire to save that horse.''

Alcina knew the bartender only by sight and reputation since she didn't frequent the Silver Slipper. And after the altercation between him and Bart over

Josie, Alcina had to admit that she was surprised to see him on the Curly-Q at all.

"Nice that someone appreciated my effort," she muttered, wondering if he'd been eavesdropping on her and Reba.

Then, thinking of the way Reed had lit into her, Alcina glanced around until she spotted the aggravating man over by the corral, deep in conversation with Moon-Eye. The grizzled ranch hand was shaking his head as if in denial. Undoubtedly, Reed was questioning Moon-Eye about being in the barn prior to the fire, as he'd intended.

Not feeling very warm toward Reed at the moment—he could have said *something* positive about what she'd done—Alcina turned back to the bartender, whose clothing appeared to be ruined.

"It looks as if you went all out, putting yourself on the line," she said, surprised by the fact. Maybe he was trying to make up for that altercation with Bart over Josie, though that had been quite a while ago when he'd been brand-new in town. "And my name is Alcina, by the way, not ma'am. That's my mother."

Ruskin laughed. "Alcina, then." Strong white, predatory teeth flashed from a soot-streaked face that was rugged and interesting, if not handsome. "I didn't get nearly as close as you did to that fire," he admitted. "I simply pitched in like everyone else to stop it from spreading."

Not *everyone,* Alcina thought, remembering Cardona's spotless appearance. Not quite.

"I admire a woman with spirit," Ruskin was saying.

"Pardon?"

"I admire you," he clarified, stepping closer, leaving her with too little room. "And I'd like to get to know you better. Maybe I could interest you in sharing supper with me some night this week."

She was not a small woman, but he was the kind of man who filled a doorway. He made her feel delicate, and the comparison didn't leave her comfortable. Or maybe it was the way he was staring at her expectantly. The strange glitter in his nearly colorless eyes suddenly reminded her of a reptile setting sights on its prey.

She took another step back to set a definite boundary. But having been raised with a certain standard of manners, Alcina thought to turn him down politely.

"I'm very flattered, Mr. Ruskin—"

"Hugh. Mr. Ruskin is my stepdaddy," he said, echoing her.

Alcina forced a smile and started to say, "I just am not—" when she was interrupted yet again.

"Ready to go home?"

This time it was Reed, who inserted himself between her and the other man. Truth be told, she was relieved that she didn't have to turn Ruskin down directly.

"Ah," the bartender said, his visage darkening. "I see how the wind blows."

As far as she knew, Alcina thought, the wind wasn't blowing anywhere. And she wasn't even sure she wanted it to. She wasn't about to argue the point when all she felt was relief. But Reed didn't have to be aware of that.

"I'll let you know, *Hugh,*" Alcina said in a purposely sweet tone meant to aggravate Reed.

Though she thought the bartender was going to say

more, he merely gave the other man an even darker look and backed off.

Before Reed could say anything, Alcina challenged him. ''What was that all about?''

''I didn't mean to get in the middle of anything,'' he muttered, suddenly appearing uncertain. ''I thought I would take you home.''

''Well, you thought wrong. I have my own vehicle.''

''Which you shouldn't drive...just in case.''

''In case what?'' she asked. ''In case we have a blue moon? That's not until next week.''

He frowned at her. ''Are you always so prickly when someone is trying to be nice to you?''

''Sorry, I didn't get the nice part. Thank you, then, but I can see myself home.''

He gave her a look that told Alcina he probably wanted to strangle her. Then he tipped his hat and backed off, leaving her staring after him.

''Things not going so good with Reed?''

The whisper in her ear startled Alcina. At least that's the excuse she gave herself for her pulse threading so unevenly as she gave Josie a weak smile.

''As best as can be expected, I suppose.''

''Don't give up yet,'' Josie insisted.

''There's nothing to give up on.''

''Okay-y-y. Then let me put it another way. Don't use Hugh Ruskin as a way to get over Reed.''

''There's nothing to get over!'' Alcina insisted, annoyance growing. And though instinct had told her to keep her distance from the bartender, she asked, ''You haven't made peace with Ruskin, I expect.''

''That creep?'' Josie shivered visibly and wrapped

her arms around her middle. "I'll never make peace with a womanizer and bully, and he'll never change."

Glad she had listened to her own intuition, Alcina said, "I thought it was weird when I saw him here in the first place."

"Chance hired him. He didn't know anything about what happened between Ruskin and me and Bart because he wasn't around at the time. Bart didn't find out about Ruskin being on the spread until this morning, and he didn't want to spoil the day by objecting. Besides, he figured Ruskin wouldn't get out of line with him around." Josie eyed Alcina closely. "He didn't get out of line, did he?"

"No. He started by saying that he admired me for saving the horse—"

"About that—"

"Don't, Josie," Alcina said with a groan. "I've heard enough about my foolishness from Reed."

"I was merely going to thank you. Skitter's one of the new mounts I brought over from my own stock. Actually, all three in the corral were. Anyhow, Skitter is young and silly and would probably have hurt himself. I'm just sorry you got hurt."

That it was Josie's horse—one of many the Curly-Q wrangler and her late mother had bred and trained on their own small ranch—was gratifying. Josie had been through too much already in the past months.

"I'll live," Alcina said. "A stiff shoulder and bruised bottom never killed anyone."

Josie grinned. "I can testify to that, considering the number of spills I've taken working with horses."

Every muscle protesting when she moved, Alcina sighed and said, "I wasn't going to leave this early, but I need my Jacuzzi. I hate to intrude on the new-lyweds, though.''

''I sure hope Pru and Chance are having a better time than we've been having around here,'' Josie said, ''though I doubt that whatever they're doing is as exciting.''

''Don't be too sure. I gave them permission to swing from the chandeliers if they wanted.'' Almost able to picture it, Alcina laughed. ''Are you ready to go put a crimp in their honeymoon aerobics?''

Josie grinned. ''Nah, you go without me. And don't wait up.''

Alcina gave her friend a quick hug, then headed for her car. No doubt Josie wanted to spend more time with Bart, even if it wasn't a particularly pleasant time.

That's what a relationship was all about. Sharing good times and bad. Not that it always worked that way, as she well remembered.

Alcina wondered if she would ever have that kind of special relationship, one where you knew what the other person would think before he thought it. Where you didn't necessarily have to say anything, where being together was enough.

Pulling away from the buildings, she pinned Reed in her headlights, but quickly swerved her car in a different direction to avoid him.

Reed wasn't the one.

She'd settled that in her mind more than a decade ago.

NEARLY AN HOUR after his third altercation of the day with Alcina, Reed stood staring at the burned shell of a barn, whose corrugated metal roof tilted to the ground on one side. If only it could talk.

Reed was still wondering about the unidentified man whom Alcina had seen in the building not even an hour before the fire. He'd already talked to Moon-Eye, who'd said he'd been looking for dance partners at the time, not more work. Reed planned to talk to Bart and Pa about it.

The last guests, dirty and scorched, were pulling their vehicles out of the yard as Reed crossed to the house, where he suspected he'd find Pa. The day had been stressful enough on the old man's heart. At least a wedding was good stress. Reed hoped the barn burning hadn't overburdened him.

Reed detoured to check on Temporary, who once more had resorted to the floor of the pickup—scared, no doubt, by all the commotion. And once again he marveled at how the dog had taken to Alcina.

He tried not to obsess over her not letting him drive her home.

She was independent, he'd give her that. Most women would be grateful for a helping hand, but not Alcina. She had even been hard-pressed to thank him for saving her pretty hide. Nope, she certainly wasn't like other women, as she was so fond of telling him.

Entering the house, Reed went straight for the noise in the kitchen.

"Where's Bart and Pa?" he asked Felice.

The housekeeper was alone, fussing with platters and serving utensils rather than leaving cleanup for the morning and getting some rest. Her way of coping, he guessed.

"Mr. Bart drove Miss Josie home," she said. "Your father is in his quarters."

"He okay?"

She avoided his gaze. "Tonight has been hard on everyone. Perhaps you should check on Mr. Emmett for yourself."

Reed's gut tightened and the back of his throat went thick. He nodded to Felice and headed for Pa's quarters—adjoining office and bedroom.

Life with his father had been hell, but losing him was unthinkable. Reed kept hoping for some compromise. Like maybe Pa would rally and surprise everyone and live to be a kindly old codger who got a kick out of watching his sons take over the reins for him.

Yeah, fat chance.

The old-codger part Reed could see, but he wasn't certain his father knew the meaning of *kind*. As for turning over the reins…he knew he and his brothers would have to wait to wrest them from Pa's lifeless hands. Somehow, the old man always got his way.

Directly outside his father's quarters, Reed heard the telephone ring. He stopped short, then figured it couldn't be anything important. He knocked but got no invitation to enter. Had Pa even heard?

Hesitating, not certain if he should wait or let the discussion keep until morning, Reed was startled when he heard Pa shout through the thick wooden door.

"Who the hell told you the Curly-Q is up for sale?"

THIS TIME the vultures hadn't even waited a day before picking at his bones.

Emmett Quarrels gripped the receiver and shook with rage as the honey-sweet voice of some real estate agent named Marla Beth Brown drawled from the other end.

"I want to assure you, Mr. Quarrels, that Desert Sun Realty can guarantee you top dollar on your property, and—"

"I didn't ask you to guarantee nothing. But I will repeat my question in case you didn't get it the first time. Who told you the Curly-Q was for sale?"

"Why, uh…"

He'd managed to fluster her. Good.

"Someone told you to call me." Emmett leaned a hand on his desk. "I want to know who."

"I'm sorry, but I can't reveal the name of my client."

"What do you think you are? Some damn lawyer with an oath of confidentiality? Or a priest? Oh, no, you're a woman…and, honey, I never knew any woman who wouldn't talk for the right incentive. So what's yours?"

The line on the other end immediately went dead. And on his end, Emmett slammed the receiver into its cradle.

He cursed a blue streak, too, and only when he had a head of steam going did he realize he wasn't alone. Reed was standing just inside the office, his back to the door.

"What's going on, Pa?"

The breath caught in Emmett's throat and he plunked down into his desk chair. "What did you hear?" he choked out.

"Enough. You okay?" Coming closer, Reed gave him a worried look. "Your color's not too good."

"Maybe I oughta go lay down," Emmett said,

thinking of a way to escape an interrogation. "Help me to my bed, Son."

"I think you ought to settle right there for a while until your blood pressure evens out. If you want, I can call Doc Baxter."

"No, no…I—I'll be fine. I'm mad is all."

"Because someone thinks the Curly-Q is for sale?"

Emmett squirmed in his seat. Reed wasn't going to let it go, he knew it. Next thing, he'd have his brothers in on the act and all three of them would be hammering at their poor old pa for the truth.

Unless…

"Son, did I tell you how glad I was to see you?"

"No, Pa," Reed said dryly. "You managed to skip that part."

"It was circumstance, you being late and all. But of my three boys, you're the one I counted on coming home."

"I would have thought that would be Bart."

Barton always had been a leader, true, but Reed would be the heart of the spread, Emmett thought. His middle son was the one who loved the land and ranching more than anything. Reed had some issues with his older brother, though…issues that Emmett could use to his advantage.

"Like I said, Son, I was counting on you to fix things," Emmett said as Reed took the seat across from him. "Make the spread pay for itself again. We've been plagued by bad-luck incidents."

"You mean like the fire tonight?" Reed asked. "Alcina Dale saw someone in the barn not an hour before. And I don't know about you, but I heard what sounded like a blast, and dollars to doughnuts, *that* was no accident, even if it was made to look like one."

Emmett cursed under his breath, but he still didn't volunteer more.

So Reed went on. "How many of these calls to sell the Curly-Q have you been getting, Pa?"

Too many, and Emmett couldn't handle the situation alone anymore. He couldn't lose the Curly-Q. He needed help from someone who would hang on to it as desperately as he. That's why he decided to confide in Reed.

"All right, Son, I confess I've had one of them calls every time something happens to make the financial situation around here worse."

Reed appeared thoughtful, then asked, "Have you told Bart?"

Emmett shook his head. "You're the only one."

He'd gone this far. He'd have to expose it all.

He opened the fancy box on his desk and lifted the wrinkled ecru paper from under the fine cigars he'd been forbidden to smoke both by Doc Baxter and Felice. He held the written warning as carefully as he would a snake ready to strike, when he offered it to Reed.

His son read silently, but Emmett knew every word by heart.

Quarrels—

    Take a friendly warning.

    You've had more years than you deserve being king of the Curly-Q. Put the place up for sale or suffer the consequences.

    Your livestock, your property, your life—all are in jeopardy unless you abdicate.

                       A Confidant

He remembered the fury that had filled him when he'd read the damn missive the first time. He'd crumpled it and had thrown it away. But something had made him retrieve the paper from the wastebasket. Something had made him smooth out the wrinkles and save the battered warning, setting it at the bottom of his cigar box, which was sacrosanct.

"Why have you been keeping this to yourself?" Reed asked as he set the letter on the desk between them.

"I didn't believe the warning, of course, not right away," Emmett admitted. "But whoever wrote that finally managed to convince me. No proof, though. Nothing for the authorities to go on. Someone is out to destroy the Curly-Q if I don't sell what I worked a lifetime to build."

"But you can't sell, not anymore..." Reed narrowed his gaze. "Is that why you did it, Pa? Is that why you turned the Curly-Q into a family corporation...so no one could force you to sell? Did you think that would scare off whoever has been doing this—"

"I had Howard Siles draw up them papers because I wanted my boys around me before I die!"

Reed turned ashen and clenched his jaw. Father and son stared at each other for a moment. Then Reed recovered too quickly for Emmett to be certain the boy was convinced.

"Pa, Bart is a lawman, for God's sake. So why haven't you showed this to him, or Chance?"

"And play right into the villain's hands?"

"How do you figure?"

"You think Barton wants more trouble in his life? He lost a wife to violence and he fears for his kids.

And Chance, he just needs an excuse to roll on to the next town."

"Chance is a married man now. And a father."

"So he won't want Pru or Hope in danger, neither. He'll take them with him. The way the corporation is set up, majority rules. Your brothers don't love this land and this way of life the way we do. We're alike in that, Son. Barton and Chance...I'm afraid they could outvote you..."

He'd hated that part of the deal most, but Barton had only agreed to come back if the power to say what happened on the Curly-Q was left to him and his brothers.

"You can't tell Barton or Chance, Reed. I'm warning you, that could mean the end of everything. Promise me you'll keep what I told you between us."

Emmett's heartbeat fluttered when Reed didn't promise any such thing. He gripped the chair arms and took a deep breath.

"You expect me to fix things alone?" Reed finally asked. "I wouldn't know where to start."

Air whooshed down Emmett's lungs in one long draft. "We start by making sure the bank doesn't foreclose."

"Tucker would really do that to you?"

Emmett thought about the glee his former partner and owner of the bank would have in evening an old score. "He will unless you stop him."

"And how do you propose I do that?"

"Simple." Emmett beamed as he warmed up to his plan. "You stop the old goat from foreclosing on us by marrying his daughter."

Chapter Four

"You want me to marry Alcina Dale?" an incredulous Reed asked.

"Why not? She's a fine-looking woman, like her
mama," Emmett said. "And she's smart. Resourceful. But she's also a handful as I hear it, scared off
every good man who was ever interested in her."

"So that made you think she's right for me?"

"Now, don't you get on your high horse, Son,"
Emmett said. "It's more than time you settled down
yourself and—"

"Whoa!"

But Pa was on a roll. "—got yourself a family. So
you and Alcina have something in common. It's not
natural, a woman her age being single and childless.
For a while, I thought she and Barton might make a
good match, but then Josie came along and turned his
head."

Bart again...

"Pa, you can't be serious," Reed said, even as he
grew irritated at the thought of the beautiful, spirited
blonde with his brother.

"You don't think I'm serious about hanging on to
the Curly-Q? If you and Alcina get hitched, Tucker

would never foreclose, not when this spread will be his daughter's home and part of his grandkids' future.''

"Now we're having kids?" Reed choked out.

"Alcina's a fine figure of a woman. Good child-bearing hips. Of course she'll give me more grandkids!''

Where had this spate of imagination come from? Reed wondered. He'd never shown any romantic interest in Alcina. And he'd never known his father to believe in fairy tales.

"Why, with you and Alcina as man and wife, old Tucker might even throw in the back mortgage payments as a wedding present!" Emmett enthused.

Reed was stunned. If the hopeful expression on Pa's face was any indication, he was serious. And it didn't sound as if this was a spur-of-the-moment idea. It sounded as if he'd planned it all out in detail.

Is *that* why Pa had wanted him home? Not to run the ranch—Bart's province, even though his older brother's heart wouldn't be in it—but to save the place from financial ruin through marriage?

"Alcina has something to say about who she marries..." Reed said tightly, "if she even has any interest in giving up the single life."

"You can convince her. That she's the town spinster has got to be eating away at her. And by now, that biological clock of hers should be a time bomb ready to go. A woman couldn't do better than you for a husband and father for her children, that's for certain.''

As glad as he was that Pa thought so highly of him, Reed wasn't so sure that Alcina would agree with that flattering opinion.

"But she doesn't love me."

Given that they hadn't been able to have a conversation without exchanging heated words, he guessed she might not even like him, for that matter. And why was he even having this ridiculous conversation in the first place? Reed wondered.

"And I don't love her," he added anyway.

Being interested wasn't anywhere close to the kind of emotion he should have for the woman with whom he meant to spend a lifetime.

"Romantic love isn't all it's cracked up to be, Son," Emmett said, "as I well know. I made my share of mistakes. Three disastrous marriages all because I thought I was in love." He shook his head. "Maybe a different approach to choosing a mate isn't such a bad idea. Real love, the kind that lasts forever, can grow from respect…at least, so I've been told."

"What respect?" Reed protested. "Alcina and I don't even know each other anymore."

"That can be fixed right quick," Emmett insisted. "If you want it to be, that is." His expression suddenly stricken, he stared at Reed for a moment before adding, "You don't have to decide now. Take some time to ponder on it." Then he sighed and his voice softened when he said, "Only, I suggest you don't take too long or there won't be anything to save, and I know the Curly-Q means as much to you as it did to me."

Which reminded Reed that the old man had a finite number of days left in this world. And that he himself had little time to win the approval and respect of the father who had seemed to look over him at every turn to favor Bart.

Trying not to let past hurts intrude on the present,

Reed noticed his father was absently rubbing his chest. His gut clenched.

"Pa, are you all right? Your heart—"

"Will last a while longer. At least long enough to see you make me proud. No doctor can fix what's wrong with me. Doc Baxter crabs about me taking it easy. And I *want* to be easy, especially in my mind, Son. Believe me, I want to last on this earth as long as I can. That means being able to spend my remaining days on this earth on the Curly-Q. I just need to know that you won't let me down."

The burden of his dying father's last wish resting squarely on his shoulders, Reed immediately said, "Don't worry, Pa, I won't let you down."

A rash promise he'd probably live to regret.

ALCINA GROANED as she tossed aside her crochet-trimmed sheets the next morning. Carefully, she slipped out of bed and tested her body parts. The Jacuzzi might have helped but it hadn't cured what ailed her. Her right shoulder was stiff and her left hip and buttock were bruised and sore from the fall.

Sun streamed brightly into the room and she realized she'd overslept, a fact confirmed by her clock. How could she have forgotten to set the alarm? She'd planned to make a special breakfast for Pru and Chance.

Then, again, the newlyweds might still be in bed, she thought with a grin.

After twisting her sleep-mussed hair high and securing it with a clip, Alcina jumped into the shower long enough to let some hot water pulse and pound her shoulder to loosen up the tight muscles. She supposed she'd have to make an ice pack and sit on it for relief in her other quarter. At least she was awake and feeling more energetic. In a hurry to scope out the breakfast situation, she threw on a comfortable old bathrobe and a pair of fuzzy slippers.

Heading downstairs, Alcina ran her fingertips along the carved wooden railing that she'd restored with her own hands. She derived joy from what had been a project of love for her—turning her old family home where she'd been raised into the Springs Bed-and-Breakfast.

Every detail had come from a combination of research and her own fertile creativity.

In New York, overseeing similar interior design for other vintage-property owners, ones with unlimited budgets, hadn't been nearly as satisfying. And although it was true that she'd had to make do for herself with more inexpensive replicas than antiques, she would add subsequent pieces of the real thing as time and her tight budget allowed.

Nearing the swinging door between dining room and kitchen, Alcina was lured by the scent of coffee so rich that it made her salivate. She guessed Josie had beat her to it.

But as she stepped into the kitchen, she saw only Pru on a stool at the counter, fully dressed and sipping a mug of coffee. The redhead looked thoughtful rather than sparkling, as a bride should be after her wedding night.

"Morning."

"Oh, Alcina." The furrow crossing Pru's forehead immediately smoothed out. "You're awake."

"Is Chance still asleep? I was planning on making you two a breakfast feast."

"I know, and it's so sweet of you. But Chance is

already gone. He headed out to the Curly-Q with Josie a quarter of an hour ago,'' Pru said. ''Double damnation! A fire.'' Her face paled a little, making her freckles pop. ''Now the barn has to be rebuilt. What next? Chance couldn't get back to the ranch fast enough.''

''Some bad luck, huh?''

Pru frowned again. ''A lot of that going around lately.''

''So Josie has been telling me.''

''She also told me that you were a heroine last night.''

At least everyone but Reed Quarrels believed that, Alcina thought. Though why his opinion of her should matter so much, she didn't know.

Shaking the aggravating man free of her thoughts, she said, ''I'm glad you and Chance had already left. I wouldn't have wanted anything to spoil your memories of your wedding day. Now…how about that breakfast?''

''Nothing for me, thanks. I want to get home.'' Pru slid off the stool, put her mug in the dishwasher and pulled car keys from her jeans pocket, her engagement ring sparkling, reminding Alcina of the diamond Reba had found.

''Missing your little girl already?''

Pru grinned. ''How did you guess?'' She kissed Alcina on the cheek. ''Thanks for last night, though.''

''The wedding night went well, then?''

''The details would make you blush.''

''You might be surprised—you'd have to go some.''

''Oh, we did, believe me.''

The women laughed and hugged. Then, having al-

ready hung her wedding dress in the new sport-utility
vehicle Chance had bought her for a wedding gift,
Pru left the back way, dancing around Josie's cat,
who'd come from the ironing room.

"Hey, Miss Kitty," Alcina purred.

Though the feline's real name was Peaches, Alcina
preferred the one Josie had given her in the throes of
her amnesia in her early days in Silver Springs.

"What are you looking for? Attention or food?"

From the frantic *meow,* undoubtedly both, so Alcina picked up the cat and carried her into the mudroom where she poured some fresh crunchies into a
bowl, then slid a hand down the little beast's back
and up her tail while the cat took the first bite.

Hungry herself, Alcina decided to make an omelet.
She was digging in the refrigerator, gathering ingre-
dients, when she heard someone at the back door.

"Come on in," she called.

Hands filled, she elbowed the fridge door closed
and turned to find Reed Quarrels planted in the middle of her kitchen.

The breath caught in her throat for a moment. Then
she said, "Reed...if you're looking for Chance, you
must have missed him somehow. He and Josie headed
for the Curly-Q about twenty minutes ago."

"I'm not looking for my brother. I'm here for
you."

Her pulse fluttered alarmingly, and she allowed her
gaze to drift from his Stetson to the work shirt buttoned straight to his neck, then down to the wash-
softened and faded jeans that hugged him so deli-
ciously.

Licking her lips, she lifted her gaze to find that he
was eyeing her, as well—the toppling hair, old robe,

fluffy slippers. Some sight she must make in comparison. But when their eyes met, she saw something in Reed's that made her a little light-headed.

And before she knew what happened, Alcina lost hold of an egg. It plopped right out of her hand and onto the kitchen floor.

"Great," she muttered, setting the rest down on the counter and grabbing a wad of paper towels. Self-conscious, she bent over to clean up the mess. "Go ahead and say it."

"Say what?"

"Whatever's on your mind."

Rising, Alcina could see that Reed was swallowing a smirk and trying to hide it below his pale gray Stetson. The darn hat didn't hide everything though. She knew he was laughing at her. *Again.* Red-faced, she wondered how it was that she gave him so many reasons to do so.

He said, "I was just thinking you have an unusual relationship with food."

Ridding herself of the evidence, Alcina looked Reed in the eye. Well, as best she could with him wearing the hat and all.

"So what is it that I can do for you?" she choked out, feeling pressurized by his very presence.

"It's what I'd like to do for you—thank you properly for saving the horses."

"I had the distinct impression that you thought my heroics were stupid and uncalled for."

"I was merely more worried about your safety than I was about the horses." He flicked the Stetson back from his forehead. Eyebrows arched, he asked, "All body parts functioning properly?"

"Uh...uh-huh."

And some not so properly.

What would Reed think if he knew her breasts were tightening and a warmth was rushing down her belly and along her thighs?

"When I said 'thank you properly' I meant with more than words," Reed went on smoothly. "I'd like to take you out on the spread late this afternoon."

An odd suggestion...

Suddenly realizing that she was naked beneath the robe, Alcina wrapped her arms around herself and tried to will away the sensation spreading through her like wildfire.

"If you think you'll get another good laugh at my expense, be warned that I did learn to ride when I was going to school out East," she informed him. "And I do mean ride. I even won a few ribbons jumping."

"I would never plan to make you look foolish," Reed assured her, his expression serious. "And I wasn't thinking about our going horseback riding...unless that's a deal-breaker. I had something a little different in mind."

Details of which were not forthcoming, Alcina noticed. He was waiting quietly for her answer.

Why not?

She was unable to resist the curiosity that got the best of her.

"All right. We'll play it your way, whatever that is. One question though," she said, her pulse humming merrily, but her practical brain asking for boundaries. "This outing with the two of us together, how would you define it exactly?"

"I don't understand."

Wondering if he was being purposely dense, Alcina asked, "Would you call it a …a date?"

She said the *D*-word delicately, as if that would soften the blow when he denied it.

"A date." Thoughtful for a moment, Reed nodded. "You could call it that."

Her pulse went straight to overdrive, but she wanted to kick him for making her feel so uncertain of herself. Either it was a date or it wasn't. *You could call it that*…real helpful. And now he was staring at her, his warm brown eyes filled with something that made her knees weak.

Wanting to control the situation, if not her own reaction to Reed, Alcina said, "Since it's on Curly-Q property, shall I meet you at the house?"

"The bunkhouse—my staying there is a temporary arrangement."

They settled on a time later that afternoon and then Reed took his leave. Alcina followed him only as far as the mudroom, but she watched through the back windows, Miss Kitty jumping on a work table to join her.

Reed climbed into the driver's seat of his truck with difficulty. For inside the cab, Temporary was all over him, trying to show him how much he meant to her. The dog was practically turning herself inside out with joy. Gaze pinned to the dog's activities, a far more sedate Miss Kitty growled deep in her throat.

"Oh, hush." Alcina scratched behind the cat's ears. "Temporary's not so bad. She's probably got a heart as big as her owner's."

For Reed was hugging the dog and talking to her and she in turn was licking his face and making him laugh. He certainly was even more appealing when he wasn't so serious…as long as he wasn't laughing at *her,* of course.

Continuing to watch dog and man, Alcina figured Reed would have a difficult time giving away anything that gave him that much affection and pleasure.

"Maybe that's something for me to keep in mind," she said before turning back to make her breakfast.

"THE INSURANCE ISN'T up-to-date, so we get squat there," Bart told his brothers when the three of them met in the main room of the bunkhouse a half hour later. "Pa said he couldn't afford to keep up the coverage."

"I'll pay for the materials for the new barn," Chance said, "since it was burned on my watch, so to speak."

Pouring himself a cup of coffee, Reed said, "You're not taking the blame for this one."

Not like in the old days when Chance would let himself be a scapegoat for every little thing that went wrong on the spread because Pa and Bart always expected him to be the screwup responsible. Way back then, Reed hadn't been able to understand why Chance had done that sort of thing—bad enough that he'd actually been guilty plenty of times. But now Reed saw his younger brother's actions through more knowing eyes. At least Chance had never been invisible, not the way he himself had been most of the time.

"Don't worry," Chance said, "I have the money from my rodeo winnings."

Which Reed knew Chance had wanted to use both to build a house for his family and to start a rodeo school.

"But this wasn't your fault," Reed stressed.

"But it was the fault of one of my so-called 'guests.'" Chance shook his head. "And if I hadn't agreed to have the wedding party here on the spread…"

Chance hadn't even allowed Reed to volunteer to help kick in some of his back pay. Knowing he was fighting his usual losing battle to be heard when it came to voicing his opinion around his brothers, Reed tried to cool Chance down yet again.

"You don't even know for certain that the fire wasn't accidental."

Despite what Alcina had seen and what Pa had told him, Reed didn't want Chance blaming himself.

"Yeah, I'm afraid we do know, Reed," Bart said. "I checked things out pretty thoroughly at first light. There are some definite flow patterns on the floor. The fire burned more intensely in those areas, which indicates an accelerant was used."

Though he'd suspected it was arson himself, Reed really had hoped he was wrong. "That could simply have been due to gasoline or diesel fuel being left in the wrong place."

Carefully pulling a dark object from his vest pocket, Bart asked, "Was this left in the wrong place?"

Holding it only by the edges, he set down a melted blob the size of a deck of cards in the center of the table. Reed took a closer look at the charred mess. While the object was virtually destroyed, closer inspection revealed it to be the remains of a pager.

"Who around here uses a telephone pager?" Chance asked.

"Whoever chose it as a device to set off the fire.

All the arsonist needed was a cell phone to trigger it.''

And most ranchers had cell phones, Reed knew, though Pa was a technology holdout, one of the first things Reed intended to change around the ranch. Plenty of things on the Curly-Q could use some modernizing. Some of his ideas would necessitate a considerable expenditure, cell phones being reasonable by comparison. And using them could keep an emergency in check. Or keep a hand from wasting his time riding out to deliver a message.

No doubt Vernon Martell was already using them on the VM. Would he have a pager as well? Reed wondered.

And what about Cesar Cardona? He doubted the housing developer went anywhere without one.

Both names stuck in his mind, even though he knew he had his own set of prejudices because of the land issue.

But Martell had left when the fire had started.

And Cardona had stood back and watched.

"Have you already done something to get an investigator out here?" Chance was asking Bart.

"I talked to the Taos County sheriff—I worked with John Malone a ways back. Malone says that since no one was hurt and there was no big monetary loss, an old barn isn't exactly a priority. Someone would come out, though no telling how soon." Bart shrugged and cleared his throat. "That's why I did a walk-through myself. What's left of that pager is the only thing I could find. I plan on getting it to Malone this afternoon and telling him not to bother wasting any of the county's manpower out here."

A declaration that startled Reed. True, Bart was a

seasoned lawman and had a lot of experience going over crime scenes. But how many fires had he investigated?

"Bart, don't you think you're being a little hasty?"

"I'm trying to be practical," his brother countered. "Even if an official investigator finds something that I overlooked—a big if—he's not going to put in the kind of time it takes to track down an arsonist, not without a human factor and when there's been so little property loss involved. Besides which, we need to get after cleaning up the mess and raising a new barn before the weather sets in."

So much for his opinion, Reed thought. What had he expected?

Temptation troubled him. Bart didn't know about the letter someone had sent Pa. And he didn't know about the phone calls from the realty agents, either. Would knowing make a difference? Or, as Pa had predicted, would those facts be justification to send Bart and Chance packing, agreeing to sell.

Then his own dream would be lost forever.

All considered, Reed didn't see the harm in keeping his silence a while longer.

Chance was turning the charred remains of the beeper with a pencil. "What do you hope to find from this thing—certainly not fingerprints."

"Maybe some kind of identification left inside that could lead us to the owner."

"Not likely, is it?"

"It's all we have right now."

"No, it's not," Reed countered. He locked gazes with Bart. "Alcina saw someone in the barn about a half hour before the fire."

"Why didn't you say so before this?"

"You didn't give me the opportunity. Alcina thought it was Moon-Eye doing some chores. She didn't get a good look at the man, unfortunately. I already quizzed the old buzzard and he says he wasn't anywhere near the barn all night. I thought we could start asking around, maybe find out who *did* do a disappearing act."

By now, Bart's face was dark red. "If you knew this, why the hell did you pretend you thought it was an accident?" he practically shouted.

Reed didn't blink. "Maybe I thought someone should play devil's advocate."

"Someday you're going to have to choose a side, Reed."

"I *have* chosen a side. Ours. We're in this together, aren't we?"

Words that resonated for Reed as they cut the gab-fest and got to work on clearing up the fire debris.

Hard, dirty work. The three of them.

Together.

But for how long?

ALCINA WAS DRESSED and straightening up the parlor by the time her next visitor arrived.

Opening the door, she registered surprise. "Reba, hi. Come on in."

She stood back to let the café owner enter and smelled the distinct odor of whiskey. The normally sunny Reba looked terrible, and she was holding her cheek, which seemed a bit swollen.

"Are you all right?"

"I think it's an abscess," Reba mumbled. "Tooth's been bothering me off and on since yesterday morning. Now it's just on. I'm on my way to Taos to see the dentist.''

Which explained her drinking this early. No doubt Reba had been using the whiskey medicinally, to cut the ache.

"What brings you here?" Alcina asked.

"The diamond. I could hardly get to sleep last night with it still in my possession," Reba admitted. "I want to give it to Pru for safekeeping. I mean, it was lost at her wedding. When the owner finally realizes it's gone, Pru will be the one who hears about it."

"But she's already left for home."

"Darn!" Reba winced. "I'm late as it is, and I don't want to carry something so valuable around with me."

"I could hold it for you, maybe get it to Pru later."

"Would you? Honey, you're a gem yourself."

The café owner started to laugh at her own joke, then grimaced when the laughter obviously caused her more pain. Rubbing her swollen cheek with one hand, she used the other to pull a zipped plastic bag from her pocket.

"At least that's off my mind," Reba mumbled as Alcina took it from her. "Thanks, honey."

"No problem. I'm sure the mystery will all be taken care of by the end of the day. You have no reason to worry."

"I hope you're right."

After Reba left, Alcina couldn't help but lift the diamond from the plastic bag for a better look. Moving closer to a window, she turned the triangular-shaped gem in the sunlight and looked deep into the facets.

But no truths were bared to her.

No name…no face…no insight as to the diamond's owner.

Popping the gem back into the plastic bag, she considered where she could store it for safekeeping until she could get it to Pru.

Chapter Five

Alcina tried keeping her nerves in check when she arrived at the bunkhouse later that afternoon.

A date with Reed...

You could call it that...

Okay, so it was sort of a date. Maybe.

Even though they wouldn't be riding horseback, she'd donned her gray snakeskin boots in case he wanted to do any walking. The rest of her outfit was feminine but understated—long, flowing dark gray skirt, plain grayish-pink silk shirt and a heavy medium-gray cardigan. That way, she was ready for anything, she hoped.

At least in the way of weather...

Reed was still a question.

Alcina wasn't certain why he'd issued the invitation. A verbal thank-you had been enough. He had, after all, pulled her out of the corral, possibly saving her life. She had more for which to be grateful than he. The ranch might be part his, yes, but the horses had belonged to Josie. And he hadn't been altogether approving of her decision to go after them in the first place.

Obviously, this was his way of apologizing for giving her such a hard time. He could have sent her flowers as a grand gesture, but, clearly, he'd wanted this to be personal, which made her very, very nervous.

One look at the burned-out barn when she got out of her car was enough to make Alcina's stomach knot, especially knowing that someone might have set that fire purposely, and if so, that person had been a wedding guest.

But to what end? Revenge? Downright meanness?

She turned her back on the memory and on the skeletal building and approached the open doorway of the bunkhouse.

Not wanting to encroach on anyone's privacy, she stayed her ground at the stoop and called out, "Reed?"

"Be right there."

He came from the room to the right and was preceded by Temporary, who was looking better already. The dog's ear was on the mend and she had a sparkle to her brown eyes where before there had been suspicion.

Reed's brown eyes sparkled, as well. He gave her a slow, spine-tingling, approving once-over.

"You look so elegant. I've always admired that about you," he said.

Leaving her speechless.

Alcina hadn't even known Reed had so much as noticed her existence before the wedding.

"You look pretty nice yourself," she told him.

He smelled freshly scrubbed and he'd changed into a pair of newer jeans and a deep gold shirt with orange insets that set his still-damp hair ablaze. The shirt, as always, was buttoned clear to his neck.

From behind his back he withdrew a flower. "I thought this would look nice in your hair."

Before Alcina could take it from him, he moved in to surround her with his arms. He was standing so close, she forgot to breathe. She felt his fingers on her head as he tucked the stem through the twisted strands. Sensation rippled through her and her hair nearly stood on end. Then he moved back, his eyes bedeviling her as he admired his handiwork.

"Beautiful," he said. Quiet for a moment, long enough to stretch Alcina's nerves taut, he finally asked, "Are you ready to go?"

"I'm here, aren't I?" she said all in a whoosh. "Go where?"

"I told you, out on the spread."

"You couldn't be more specific?"

"Nope."

He grabbed his jean jacket and Stetson from a peg next to the door. Putting on the hat, he stepped outside.

Alcina eyed Reed's dusty truck sitting out front and thought about suggesting they take her car, but of course that was anything but practical. She didn't have a four-wheel drive and there were no real roads on most of the ranch. They'd be driving over dirt, gravel or solid rock, and that's not an even surface. Her car would never make it. She stepped toward his vehicle, but Reed hooked a hand at her elbow and turned her, the dog running before them, making it a threesome.

"I thought we could compromise."

"Compromise is good," Alcina murmured, wondering what in the world he meant.

She avoided looking at the burned-out hulk as they

followed the length of the bunkhouse, but she couldn't stop herself from shuddering.

If it hadn't been for Reed…

As if he knew exactly how she felt, he slipped a reassuring arm around her back, but whatever he was thinking, he kept it to himself.

When they rounded the bunkhouse, the two quietly waiting horses tacked in tandem took her by surprise. As did the wagon behind them.

"Good Lord, where did you find that old thing?" she asked, a chord of pleasure making her pulse hum.

"Right here on the property, though only God knows the last time it was actually put to use."

Reed helped her up and into the seat, which he'd covered with a beautifully worked quilt. She touched the hand-stitched material and wondered who had made the piece and how long ago. It was a work of art, revealing someone's love for the Southwest via cloth-worked mesas and horses and adobe buildings.

She wondered if Reed had chosen to use it because he knew she appreciated beautiful old things, or it had been as simple as his wanting to pad her from an assuredly bumpy ride while protecting her clothes.

Reed threw his jacket into the back and climbed up on his side, then reached forward to pick up the reins. Alcina couldn't help but admire the muscles that rippled along his shoulders and upper arms, muscles built naturally from hard work rather than from lifting health-club weights.

When Temporary launched herself into the back of the wagon, Alcina turned to greet the dog only to see her bound over a huge picnic basket and a smaller cooler. The animal parked herself directly behind Reed.

"Uh-oh," Alcina murmured, realizing they were to have a picnic supper somewhere on the property. "You wouldn't have brought barbecue ribs along?"

"Not a one."

"Thank goodness!"

They laughed companionably and Temporary barked as Reed clucked to move the horses off.

Happily surprised by the wagon ride, her tension released by the shared laughter, Alcina sat back as Reed expertly took them away from all signs of civilization. She ignored the bumps in the ride and took pleasure in the fresh air and deepening turquoise sky. And gradually she became aware of horses following them—including the one Josie called Skitter—but mostly the same nosy band that hung around the road and escorted visitors to the house.

Which prompted her to ask, "So how come you're not staying at the main house?"

"Daniel is using my old bedroom," Reed said. "And Lainey is in Chance's. Bart and his kids are used to having a whole house to themselves. This is already a big compromise for them, so I wouldn't want them to double up for me. I'm fine in the bunkhouse for the moment, but while Frank Ewing is currently the only hand there, we'll have to hire a few more men before spring. So like I said, it's only temporary."

"Until…?"

"Until my own domicile arrives tomorrow."

"You're moving a house from the ranch where you worked?" an incredulous Alcina asked.

"A trailer." He grinned. "It's not fancy, but I like having my own place."

"No matter where you go, it's home."

"Right," he agreed. "I bought it several years back when I got a big bonus at the end of a season. Actually, this is only the second time I'm moving the trailer, and hopefully the last." He looked at her thoughtfully enough to send an expectant shiver up her spine. "If things work out the way I expect, I'll be moving into something more permanent very soon, anyway."

More permanent had a nice ring to it, Alcina decided. That meant Reed would continue to be around. She tried shoving away the slight edge she kept experiencing around him and told herself to relax already.

For the rest of the short ride, they talked about the recent past. About her fixing up the bed-and-breakfast. About his running someone else's spread. More than she'd ever heard Reed talk in her life.

In the past, he'd always been quiet, both as a boy and as a young man, not at all open. Alcina guessed his living away from his family must have brought about some changes.

By the time they reached the bend in the river where Reed pulled the wagon to a halt, she felt as if they knew each other. Almost. At least a little.

The spot he'd chosen was picture-perfect. The water rushed and foamed over big rocks in the bed. The riverbank was laced with cottonwoods. And cypress and juniper bushes dotted the rimrock that rose behind them, its blazing red reflecting the setting sun.

"How lovely," Alcina murmured, and Temporary barked her agreement as she went racing after a rabbit.

Reed merely smiled and spread the quilt over a patch of grass while she twirled around like a girl and lifted her face to the late-autumn sky. Soon the land would turn harsh with the winter snows and reveal a different sort of beauty. Each season in New Mexico was special to her.

Though she was very much like her mother in some ways—taste in art and music and personal style—Alcina felt far more connected to the elements here than on the East Coast.

Alcina guessed Silver Springs would always be the home of her heart.

Reed hauled out the picnic basket and she investigated the contents while he went back to the wagon for the cooler. She removed plastic and paper goods, then from below, warm food wafting heavenly aromas.

Temporary shot out of nowhere and sat at the edge of the quilt, liquid brown eyes alert for castoffs.

Alcina suspected Felice had outdone herself when she uncovered a glass dish to find a layered chicken-and-cheese-enchilada casserole with sour-cream topping. Her mouth immediately watered and she opened another package containing corn-bread sticks, also still warm.

Reed set down the cooler next to the basket and him next to her. He popped the cooler top and added to the mix a plastic container filled with Southwestern salad—black beans and corn and peppers.

"Wine or fancy water?" he asked.

"Both, please."

She dished out the food, a plate each for the three of them. He poured the drinks.

After leaning forward to give the dog her treat, Alcina glanced up even as Reed opened the wine, the bottle appearing almost delicate in his work-callused hands. Wondering what it would be like to feel those hands stroke her length so carefully, she flushed and placed her focus back on the food where it belonged.

You could call it a date...

While she certainly would like to, she didn't even know if he had a romantic intention in his head.

"Here you go."

"What? Oh..." Taking the glass from him, she said, "I've never thought of you as the wine type."

"Hmm, beautiful *and* perceptive." He pulled out a beer and held it up in toast. Once they got settled, glasses and plates full, Reed asked, "So, are you happy with your life exactly as it is?"

"Things could always be better, I guess," Alcina said, taking a bite of the casserole. "Oh, this is delicious." A sip of wine and she sighed, then went back to the conversation. "I have my complaints like everyone else, but, yes, on the whole, I feel very lucky. You?"

"I have my complaints." He grinned and washed down a mouthful of food with a slug from the beer bottle. "But I love what I do. I couldn't imagine anything could be more satisfying than ranching. I have this attachment to the land—"

"Just like your father."

When he didn't respond, she wondered if he took that as a criticism. They ate in silence for a few minutes. Feeling the edge of her hunger satisfied, Alcina gave the watchful dog another treat, then went back to her wine.

His plate nearly empty, Reed asked, "The East Coast didn't suit you?"

The circumstances, especially those surrounding her relationship with Jeffrey, hadn't suited her, but

Alcina didn't want to ruin a perfect meal with that discussion.

So she merely said, "Life there wasn't all that it was cracked up to be," and took one last forkful of salad before giving up, at least temporarily. She set the plate to her side, where the dog could get it. "My brother loves it. And Mother moved back, as well. She and Daddy haven't officially separated, but…"

Reed digested that before asking, "You went to live with your mother's people while you went to school, right?"

"Right," she said, thinking Reed was awfully curious about her past. "My aunt and her family. They were wonderful to me. And I loved interior design—an art in itself. I learned how to put things together, to create sometimes from very little, to make an interesting or beautiful space."

"*You're* beautiful…and messy as usual." Reed reached over to rub at her chin. "Just a little sour-cream sauce this time."

He sucked it off the pad of his thumb. Mesmerized by his unconscious action, Alcina couldn't tear her eyes away from his mouth.

"Did you get it all?" She was trying to sound natural, but she noted the hitch in her voice.

"Let me take a closer look."

Alcina's eyes widened as Reed slid his hand around the back of her neck. The calluses left behind a trail of gooseflesh and a raggedy pulse. He hesitated long enough that she had the chance to back off if she wanted.

Pulse rushing so that she could hear it, Alcina sat frozen, waiting to see what came next.

"Don't think I quite got it all," he murmured, serious brown eyes staring deep into hers.

Alcina's eyelashes fluttered as he moved closer. Feeling his breath on her face, she made a little sound at the back of her throat, sort of like a squeak. But when he touched the tip of his tongue to the area in question, her sigh was one of pure pleasure.

Waves and waves of warmth swam through her, followed by a tension like none she'd ever known except in the full throes of sex.

Then Reed's mouth brushed hers. Alcina closed her eyes and parted her lips. And waited. Seconds seemed to pass as slowly as aeons. Like the beating of a clock, her heart ticked out several seconds before his mouth melded with hers.

Unable to trust her own senses, feeling as if she was dreaming the kiss, Alcina waited again to see where it would lead. Reed slipped an arm down her back to pull her closer. His fingers splayed across her spine; she felt every one of them. He deepened the kiss and, still half-disbelieving, she sighed and went with the flow of lovely sensation flooding her as his tongue dipped into her mouth and found hers.

She met him then, kiss for kiss, touch for touch.

Upon wrapping a hand around his neck and sliding her fingers up through his thick hair, she left her side exposed. His hand drifted up from her waist and under her sweater to the edge of her breast. Her nipple tightened even before he found it through the silk and lace coverings.

His turn to moan.

Her turn to wonder if he planned to make love to her right here in the open…

Her heart thundered.

Would she dare?

He rolled the hard nub of her breast between forefinger and thumb...all it took to ready her for anything. Tension built in her as fast as lightning could strike and liquid warmth pooled between her thighs.

Squeezing her legs together to battle the discomfort, she tried to think. Tried to decide.

But Reed didn't give her that opportunity. He simply stopped.

Stopped fondling her breast.

Stopped kissing her.

Stopped *her* from losing her head!

He let go of her and straightened himself so fast that Alcina nearly fell back against the quilt. Stunned at the abrupt end to the hot embrace, she caught herself both figuratively and mentally. But she could do nothing about the inner physical ragings that wouldn't subside on command.

What now?

"I didn't mean for that to happen," Reed said quietly.

"Oh."

Heat crept from her middle to her extremities. Not the heat of passion this time, but one of embarrassment.

"I mean, it's not that I didn't enjoy it, but that I didn't bring you out here to...to..."

Reed didn't finish. He didn't have to. Alcina got the picture.

"No problem. I'm not insulted, if that's what you're worrying about." Merely abashed at her easy abandon. She put a light sophisticated spin to something that meant more to her than she was willing to let him comprehend. "I mean, we are two adults with healthy libidos.'' She forced a smile and lied, ''It was only a kiss.''

At least for him it had been, so she would let him off the hook. If only she hadn't responded so mindlessly...so thoroughly...she wouldn't feel this horrible sense of building humiliation now.

Temporary had moved around to Reed's other side and was nudging him and pretending that Alcina didn't exist.

Ingrate!

''Good girl,'' Reed murmured. ''Now go lie down.''

Alcina assumed he meant the dog.

As did Temporary, who followed orders and returned to the foot of the quilt.

What now?

''Are you comfortable out here?'' Reed suddenly asked.

''Absolutely,'' Alcina lied. She didn't know whether or not she'd ever be comfortable around him again. ''The air is starting to get crisp, but—''

''That's not what I meant. On the land. *This* land. The Curly-Q. Could you ever feel at home here?''

''I sort of do already,'' she admitted tightly.

Alcina wanted nothing more than to get off the damn land right this moment. Or crawl into a hole where he couldn't see her. But that wasn't going to happen. She would have to make the best of things for a little while longer. Then she would find some excuse to get out of here and would never have to see Reed again. Well, practically never. He was the brother of her best friend's husband.

At least she would never have to be alone with him after this.

What had she been thinking?

Alcina fetched her wineglass and took a long swallow as Reed asked, "So, a ranch appeals to you?"

"I never spent much time on the Curly-Q when Bart and I were in school together." She was on automatic, part of her acting as natural and social as possible, other part wondering how to get out of this situation and fast. "And I did always live in town. But the beauty of the landscape in this part of the country is what drew me back to New Mexico in the first place."

At least he wasn't asking her anything personal.

"So I assume you're making Silver Springs your permanent home?"

"That is the plan," she mumbled.

"Any other plans for your future?"

"What do you mean?"

She raised her glass to her lips as Reed asked, "How do you see yourself? Single? Married?"

Alcina nearly spit the wine over them both, but miraculously swallowed fast instead. "Married would be nice, but first there would have to be a man who would interest me in that way...not to mention one who was interested in return."

A concept she didn't want to examine too closely at this exact moment.

"I'm interested," Reed said. "What about you?"

Certain their wires had somehow crossed, she echoed, "Interested?"

Silent, he stared at her.

Edgy, she squirmed inside. Her heart began to tick again, like a bomb on a timer.

So when he said, "Would you be interested in marrying me?" the bomb went off.

Little ripples of internal explosions leaving Alcina too light-headed to speak.

Cruelty had never been one of Reed's vices as far as she knew, if, indeed, he had any vices at all. So what was this? Had she misheard him?

Unable to voice that question, Alcina merely brayed like a jackass.

To which Reed frowned.

Her unnatural laughter faded. "C'mon, Reed!" she gasped.

"I'm serious."

He appeared to be serious.

Suddenly, Alcina could hardly breathe. Not the kind of wonderfully passionate breathless that came with deep looks and a stirring kiss. But the kind that threatened to cut off her air supply for good.

"I—I don't get it."

"I know this is coming out of nowhere…and yet not," he insisted, looking out toward the horizon rather than at her. "We've known each other forever. Neither one of us is getting any younger and we're both still single."

Alcina almost interrupted him then, almost told him about Jeffrey, but Reed didn't give her the opportunity.

"It's more than time that I thought about a family. You, too. And we're both set on staying put in a place where the pickings are slim," he added.

Which made Alcina wince.

Slim pickings—how flattering, she thought—no one had ever referred to her charms in quite that way before.

"And it makes sense," Reed went on. "You and

me, I mean. After all, our fathers were partners once upon a time, so why not us?''

He still wasn't looking at her.

''Partners,'' she repeated. ''You make it sound like a business deal.''

Her breath came back in a whoosh and her heart settled into a less jagged beat.

''I guess you could think of it as a business deal of sorts,'' he said, finally meeting her horrified gaze. He went on. ''We're two sensible, mature people who know what they want and can work together to make it happen.''

Reed seemed pleased with himself. Really pleased.

Alcina just wanted to scream.

You could think of it as a business deal!

This wasn't Alcina's first marriage proposal. Actually, it wasn't the first time business had been involved, though she hadn't known that about Jeffrey Van Ack when he'd set out to sweep her off her feet. No, none of that ''sweeping'' for down-to-earth Reed. He simply wanted a home and family. At least he was honest, she'd give him that.

And his proposal certainly was the one she'd never be able to forget.

No matter that she might like to…

''So, what about it?'' Reed pressed, reaching out and capturing one of her hands between his. His expression serious, he said, ''Alcina Dale, will you be my partner in life?''

Affronted, Alcina wanted to tell Reed no. She wanted to pull her hand away and smack him and inform him that, if he was the last man on earth, she wouldn't marry him.

The only problem was, her doing so might be the biggest mistake of her life.

Josie's words from the wedding came back to haunt her. *Real love doesn't come around that often. And neither does a good man, as I very well know. So if you want Reed and you get a shot at him, take it. If you don't, you'll always wonder what might have been.*

She did want a shot at Reed Quarrels, Alcina realized. That was what she'd always wanted, no matter that she'd gone looking for love in all the wrong places when she hadn't so much as won Reed's attention.

Well, she had his attention now.

And he certainly had hers.

And if she didn't act fast, she would lose it. Forever. He might be attracted to her, but he didn't love her. She knew that. If he was so determined to marry that he would ask a woman he didn't love to be his wife, he would merely find another if she rejected him now. And then she would never have a shot at what she used to dream about when she lay awake at night.

Schoolgirl dreams were so innocent, Alcina remembered, and part of her wanted to recapture that innocence. Wanted to turn a youthful dream into a mature reality.

Wanted to make Reed love her.

As crazy as it seemed after all these years, she did still feel love for him, if not the wild and crazy passion of her youth. And he was a good man, not a cheat. One who wouldn't lie to get what he wanted.

They could have a partnership, but unlike that of their fathers before them, something solid on which they could build a future.

Perhaps she could even make him fall in love with her...

Praying that she wasn't making the biggest mistake of her life, Alcina said, "All right, Reed, I accept. I would be honored to be your partner in life."

UNDER THE DARK OF NIGHT, he set out to retrieve his diamond.

The stone could betray him, which would mean that, if its ownership came to light, he'd have to run, and after all his hard work.

He wouldn't let anyone ruin this for him—anyone meaning a Quarrels.

His plans had been too well laid; he was so close to success that he could almost taste it. Therefore, he meant to retrieve the stone and have it remounted before its absence could be noted.

The bigmouthed bitch had already spread the word about where she'd found the diamond. At least she hadn't gone around advertising the unusual cut or the size. To claim it, the person would have to know that it was a two-and-a-half-carat trillion. If anyone put things together, that the stone belonged to him but that he'd been nowhere near the entrance of the barn fighting the fire with the other guests, he'd be exposed.

Luckily for him, Reba Gantry worked nights and her house stood alone at the end of a mostly deserted lane several blocks from Main Street and her café. Even so, he took no chances, used no vehicle that could alert watchful eyes.

One with the night, he sneaked toward her house like the thief he had become.

Getting inside was easy, the back door was unlocked. In these parts, hardly anyone worried about intruders. What fools they were.

A single lamp lit the living room. He stood there for a moment, letting his eyes adjust to the light, trying to imagine where Reba might have hidden the diamond for safekeeping. Not here on the first floor. For some reason, he was certain of that.

Upstairs, then, in her bedroom.

A moment later he was outside the door. It stood open, and a soft golden light on a bedside stand guided him inside.

He began with the chest, but he'd barely pawed through the lacy garments in the top drawer when he heard a noise behind him. He whipped around, shocked to see Reba herself standing in the doorway, barefoot and clad only in a low-cut nightgown. From the faint sound behind her, he suspected she'd just come from the bathroom.

"What are you doing here, honey?" she asked, her voice low and slightly slurred. "No one invited you tonight."

"Aren't you glad to see me, anyway?" he asked, swiftly moving toward her before she could scream.

But if Reba had any thoughts of screaming, she wasn't acting on them. She swayed in the doorway, and shook her head as if to clear it. He smelled the booze on her; she'd been drinking. Reba had always liked her nightcaps.

"Still mad at you," she said. "Shouldn't be here."

"Neither should you. What are you doing home from the café so early?" he asked, worried that she might not be alone for long.

"Didn't work tonight. Not feeling good." She

squinched her eyes and held the side of her face. "Ooh, my tooth…"

"You're in pain?" he asked sympathetically. "Is there anything I can do?"

"The pills they gave me," she mumbled. "Couldn't find them. And the whiskey isn't making the pain go away."

He looked around, caught sight of a bottle and highball glass on one nightstand. And there, on the floor nestled half under the bed, looked to be a pharmaceutical bottle.

Perfect.

"There it is," he murmured as she swayed and clung to the doorway to hold herself upright. "I'll get it for you."

He retrieved the narcotic and shook several pills into his hand. Then he fetched the highball glass and added a bit more booze before asking, "Say, did you ever find the owner of that diamond?"

"No, but it's not my problem anymore. Gave it to a friend for safekeeping." She frowned when he held out the glass in one hand, pills in the other. "Maybe I should wait…the whiskey…"

He knew only a moment's regret as he said, "Don't worry, it'll be okay. I'll take good care of you, Reba. You won't have to be in pain much longer."

And the combination of pain medication and alcohol would loosen her tongue.

Too easily reassured, Reba gave him a grateful smile as she accepted the means of her own destruction.

Chapter Six

On Thursday morning, Pru's father returned to Silver Springs to preside over Reba Gantry's funeral. The Reverend Brewster Prescott normally only drove the hour back to his old hometown two Sundays a month to hold a service in the small church that had once been the center of his life. The funeral was his second visit this week, his daughter's wedding having been the first and far happier occasion.

Alcina knew Reverend Prescott didn't mind the inconvenience because he had been fond of Reba, just as had they all. Everyone from town and from the surrounding ranches had turned out to bid her farewell.

Well, almost everyone, Alcina amended, still not seeing the one man who should be there.

"I don't see Cesar Cardona anywhere," she whispered to Pru as they assembled around the grave site directly behind the church. "I know they had a fight and he stomped off the other night, but you would think that Reba's death would erase any hard feelings."

"I still can't believe she's dead," Pru said, tears filling her eyes as fast as she could wipe them away.

Pru had worked as a waitress for Reba for the last two years, ever since she'd quit nursing school when she'd found herself alone and pregnant with Chance's child. She'd been in charge of the café the night that Reba had overdosed.

The café was closed now and would remain that way until the dead woman's niece and only heir arrived and decided what she wanted to do with the place. The young woman had made some innocuous excuse about why she couldn't get away to attend her aunt's funeral. For that, Alcina knew the niece would receive a cold reception from the good citizens of Silver Springs, her included.

"I must have been the last one around here to see Reba alive," Alcina said, even more deeply saddened that the woman had died the very same night that Reed had proposed. "I wish…"

"You couldn't have known. There was nothing you could do."

"No."

Somehow, though, Alcina thought the two events would stick in her mind forever, morbidly intertwined.

Hopefully, Reba's untimely death wasn't a bad omen for her upcoming marriage. She and Reed were to have a small, private ceremony and reception on Sunday. Thirteen people in all, including the Reverend and Mrs. Prescott, who would drive out yet again. Reed's family with the exception of his mother, who was tending to a sick husband in Phoenix. Her own father would be present, of course, since he lived in Taos. But her mother, Nancy, was traveling with friends somewhere in France and incommunicado, and her brother Charles, who spearheaded a financial operation in Boston, had to chair the company's annual meeting that would run through the weekend.

In the meantime, Alcina had hardly found a moment to speak to her fiancé. Reed had been too busy working. What had she expected? Their relationship was based on business rather than romance.

Still, he could have found some time to be alone with her.

Reed had brought her to the church that morning, true, but he'd been with his brothers since. They and three other men from the town were the coffin bearers.

Reverend Prescott waved over a few stragglers. ''C'mon, gentlemen, we're ready.''

Alcina glanced over her shoulder to see a couple of old cowboys. Still no Cesar Cardona.

''What was she thinking?'' Pru murmured despondently. ''Taking narcotics with alcohol.''

Alcina had witnessed Reba using whiskey to soothe the abscessed tooth. Obviously, her good sense had been dulled. She'd been unable to make a clear-headed choice when the dentist had prescribed her the painkillers. Or…

''Reba wasn't depressed, was she?'' Alcina whispered.

''No! She didn't commit suicide,'' Pru insisted. ''Not Reba. She didn't realize the danger.''

Indeed, the medical examiner had declared Reba Gantry's death to be accidental.

No reason to blow it up into something else.

Still, Alcina had a difficult time concentrating on the short prayer offered by Pru's father. Before she knew it, Reed, Bart, Chance, Hugh Ruskin and two young cowboys—newcomers whose names escaped her—were lowering the coffin into the grave.

The mourners said their last goodbyes and started back for the church to share a potluck supper.

Halfway up the incline, Alcina hesitated and turned for one last look.

A few stragglers were leaving the grave site. One man remained. He dropped a single red rose onto the coffin and paused there, head hung as if in prayer.

Alcina started.

She hadn't been aware that Vernon Martell had known Reba Gantry all that well. He'd probably eaten at her café, of course, but beyond that…well, the man was married, even if Lettie Martell was an invalid. Alcina looked around, but of course Mrs. Martell wasn't present.

She shifted uncomfortably, wondering what the rose meant.

Martell lifted his head, his gaze meeting hers. Some fleeting expression that she couldn't define crossed his features. Then it was gone. And so was he.

He whirled around and stalked between grave sites to his vehicle.

How odd.

Alcina quickly joined the women, who were setting out the communal supper, mostly covered dishes and Jell-O molds. She and Pru set up the coffee table.

"You'll never guess what I saw," she said quietly. "Vernon Martell leaving a rose on Reba's coffin."

Pru made a face.

"Do you know something I don't?"

"Yeah. Reba liked men. I mean, she really liked them."

"Even married ones?"

Pru shrugged. "I'm not sure a wedding ring meant much to her. Oh, double damnation, I'm not sure who she kept company with and who she didn't. What does it matter, anyway? She's dead, for heaven's sake!"

The mention of *wedding ring* sparked Alcina's memory. Somehow, the diamond's existence had escaped her with the news of the café owner's death. But once reminded, she told Pru all about Reba's visit.

"I heard about her finding it, of course," Pru admitted. "But no one has said anything to me about losing a stone."

"I can hardly believe it," Alcina murmured. "That diamond is at least two carats and, considering the unusual cut and clarity, must be worth close to ten thousand dollars."

Though diamonds didn't hold a particular appeal for her, she'd been around enough fine jewelry in New York to know something of what quality gems were worth.

"You'd think a woman would know if the stone fell out of her engagement ring," Pru said.

"I don't think you'd find a triangular-shaped stone in any of the engagement rings around here."

"That *would* be very unusual."

"I'd say you'd be more likely to find a cut like that in a fancy bracelet or watch or cuff links or even in a man's ring." Alcina shrugged. "Anyway, I'll get the stone later. Reba wanted me to give it to you for safekeeping."

Pru stopped and stared at her. "You've got to be kidding. With Hope and my sister Justine's three girls getting into everything, nothing is safe in that house. Do me a favor and hang on to it, would you?''

Alcina's agreement lacked the proper enthusiasm even though she figured the stone was safe enough for the time being. But what if no one ever claimed it?

A situation that made her uneasy. Someone should have claimed it by now…

"So, about your wedding," Pru said, switching topics. "Have you had that talk with Reed yet?"

The one where she told him she'd been married before, a fact that she'd buried long before returning to Silver Springs?

"Not yet."

"What are you waiting for?"

The fewer people here who knew what a fool she'd been the better, her best friend being the exception. Alcina didn't mind the title "town spinster." Better than "town fool."

Besides, what had been the point of bragging about the biggest mistake of her life and one made so long ago?

But she hadn't told any of this to the man she was about to marry on Sunday, and Reed did have the right to know, Alcina supposed. He would expect total honesty of her, even as she did of him.

"Thinking about telling him about my mistakes and doing so are two very different things," she told Pru. "It's just…too complicated to go into."

Because Reed had been directly in the center of her decision to return to New York where she'd met and married Jeffrey on the rebound, so to speak. She wasn't quite sure how rebound applied since she and Reed had never been an item. Nevertheless, she'd lost her good judgment after hearing that Reed had gotten himself engaged to a neighboring rancher's daughter.

What irony, though.

Reed hadn't actually gone through with his marriage and hers hadn't lasted a year. Alcina hadn't been able to stay married to Jeffrey once she'd understood his true intentions in pursuing her in the first place.

Love had not been involved. Business had. Her family's financial business.

The situation might be similar, but the men weren't, an uneasy Alcina reminded herself. And at least she knew where things stood this time.

Reed wasn't a cheat.

He was one of the last good, honest men.

Pru was giving her the evil eye. "I never knew you to be a coward, Alcina Dale."

"I'm not, so you can stop looking at me like that!"

But merely thinking about being honest with Reed at this point made Alcina's stomach curl and her knees weak.

What if he were to call off the wedding at the last minute?

Her uneasiness bloomed into barely controlled panic.

REED HADN'T MEANT TO PROPOSE to Alcina on their first date. He hadn't meant to marry her on their second. But it looked as if that was the way his luck was going. His sharing supper with her and his family at the funeral didn't count.

Neither did their walk home.

"Any new crises on the Curly-Q?" she asked once they were away from the graveyard.

"Not today. Not that I know of."

But the spread had experienced another bad-luck incident earlier in the week. Missing cattle. From what Pa had said, the episodes were coming closer together now, as if the perpetrator was nearing some kind of deadline.

Alcina slipped a hand around his arm to hang on to him. Her touch was firm but light. Surprised, but liking the feeling akin to one of possession, Reed enveloped her fingers with his free hand.

Her skin was smooth and silky, her fingertips soft to the touch, unlike his own work-callused pads. He absently traced a pattern along the back of her hand, and she shivered slightly.

"Chilly?"

"A little."

Guessing that to be a lie—she was wearing a dark gray wool suit and had draped herself with a wool wrap that looked like the fur of a big cat—he grinned. The thought of touching her all over in the same manner, making her quake with delicious discomfort, made him grin even harder.

But his amusement was wiped clean away when, a little breathless, she asked, "Did you ever find any of those missing cattle?"

He shook his head. "I'm afraid a couple dozen head are gone with the wind."

Not to mention the several thousand dollars they would have brought at auction.

All week, he and Bart and Chance had been frustrated by this newest invasion of their property. Someone had pulled down the fence and had backed an eighteen-wheeler right into their northernmost pasture. The tire tracks had still been there to prove it.

They'd had no idea how many head were missing

or if there was another piece of downed fence somewhere else on the property. That meant riding fence and counting head—an all-consuming task on a range the size of the Curly-Q.

"From the looks of it," Reed said, "Bart figures we've been rustled by professionals."

"Does he have any ideas about who was behind this?"

"His being a lawman doesn't make him psychic!" Reed snapped. Then, realizing Alcina had stiffened at his tone, he muttered, "Sorry, didn't mean to take it out on you. It's been a tough week. And, as good a lawman as Bart might be, tracking cattle rustlers isn't his specialty. He doesn't have the time for it, either. None of us do."

"So much money lost, though," Alcina said. "What a shame, there doesn't seem to be an end to the bad luck on the Curly-Q."

Didn't he know it.

Though Reed had hoped the cattle rustling was a stand-alone incident having nothing to do with the others, Pa had received another of the dreaded telephone inquiries from a real estate agent on the very next morning.

And, to Reed's frustration, Pa still refused to let him tell his brothers about the threat. Did Pa really think Bart and Chance hadn't figured out that someone was waging a campaign to get the land itself?

But to what purpose?

Land development? The name Cesar Cardona immediately came to mind.

Or increasing the size of someone else's spread? Like the VM Ranch owned by Vernon Martell.

Reed wouldn't doubt that his brothers were speculating, as well. Neither of them was naive enough to believe all those incidents really had been a matter of luck. Only, no one had come up with an actual theory about who or why.

And, hell, Pa could be right about his brothers, after all, Reed told himself. If they had a way out offered them, they might take the money and leave him hanging out to dry.

"Reed, about the wedding," Alcina suddenly said. "Are you sure you want to go through with it? If not, say so now, please. Let's not make another…um, a mistake."

Reed had his doubts, all right.

Here he was, less than a week after proposing, approaching what should be the most important day of his life and dreading rather than anticipating it.

Even though Alcina had agreed to marry him without the romance that most women expected in their lives, he felt as if he was cheating her because he couldn't be totally honest. Couldn't tell her that this marriage was Pa's plan to save the spread.

If Tucker Dale came through the way Pa was expecting him to, that was.

Committing himself to what could be a lost cause…Reed couldn't help having second thoughts about doing so.

But in the end, he would keep that commitment.

With all that had been going on over the past few days, he'd had neither time nor energy left over for Alcina.

"If you're worried because you haven't seen much of me until today, it couldn't be helped. I'm real sorry that I've had to leave the wedding plans strictly in your hands," he said, "as capable as I know them to be."

Alcina digested that for a moment before nodding. "I'd say yours are full right now, so don't worry about it. Everything is under control."

The wedding maybe, Reed thought, but not his life. Which had been eating at him all week.

As they approached the bed-and-breakfast, Reed casually asked, "Your father will be here, right?"

"Of course Daddy's coming. Why? Are you worried about it? I mean about our fathers being in the same place at the same time?"

"I expect Pa knows to behave himself."

"Daddy, too."

"Some fence-mending would be in order," Reed said, hoping that Alcina would volunteer to referee.

But all she said was, "I'll settle for a permanent truce." She climbed the two steps to the roofed porch that ran the length of the territorial-style building. "What ever did go wrong between them in the first place? They were partners for so many years, both in the mine and in keeping the town running. Not to mention they were best friends."

Following her onto the porch, Reed said, "I'm not sure. Probably the usual with Pa. Him getting on a high horse about something or other. Making impossible demands of your father. Trying to micromanage everything. Driving him away just like anyone who ever cared for him." Even as Pa had driven away his three wives and, later, his three sons, Reed thought. And yet another partner. "Noah Warner didn't last out the first year under Pa's thumb."

"Yes, but we don't really know that your father was at fault. Some men simply aren't cut out for hard work and Noah Warner might have been one of them,'' Alcina said. She leaned her back against a support post for the porch roof. ''Well, I'll demand that Daddy steel himself if anything that has to do with your father happens at the wedding. Or after. Surely he can give a man who's dy…uh, sick…a little leeway.''

''You can say the word *dying*.''

''Oh, Reed, I'm really, really sorry about that.''

Alcina's soft gray eyes were liquid with something that stirred him inside. Her expression held great sympathy. He'd never seen her more beautiful.

''We're all sorry about Pa.'' Reed curled his hands into fists. ''Can't hardly believe it, though. Not any of us. Not when he seems okay most of the time.''

''It's difficult to think about losing someone we love, especially a parent,'' Alcina said, moving toward him. She placed her hand on his chest, the featherlike touch stirring him. ''I want you to know that I'll be there for you, Reed. If you need something, all you have to do is ask.''

She meant that—he could hear it in her voice.

Drawn to Alcina as he had been to no other woman, Reed closed the gap between them and took her in his arms. She stayed relaxed for a moment. Then she sighed and he felt her hands slide from under his ribs around his back to encircle him. She tucked her forehead to his cheek.

A wave of tenderness washed over Reed as he held Alcina in his arms.

Tenderness…and something more stirring.

He dipped his head to brush her lips with his. A kiss of gratitude, he thought. For her understanding.

And another of apology. For his not being totally honest with her.

And a third just because he wanted to.

"Oh, Reed."

Her warm breath aroused him to kiss her yet again, this time more fully as he had on their picnic, when he'd proposed to her. She swayed against him and he tightened his hold. This felt so right, too, that it startled him.

He'd gotten carried away the day of the picnic and had almost made love to her right there and then. He didn't know what was wrong with him, but he wanted to take her again...and yet he wouldn't.

Despite the way his gut tightened and his manhood sprang to life, he knew it wouldn't be right. Guilt burdened him and he was determined to stop before it faded like the waning light already had and he did something he would regret.

So when she murmured, "Maybe we should go inside," he dropped his arms and backed off.

"It's late," he said. "I'd better get going. I need to get up with the rooster tomorrow."

As if the next day would be different from any other.

"Reed, it's not even seven o'clock."

"But I have some things to take care of back at the ranch."

Emotions warred across Alcina's fine features. Acceptance won.

"All right, then. Good night."

She whirled around and entered her home, shutting him out with the slam of her front door.

The irony of his situation didn't escape Reed.

If he didn't plan on marrying Alcina, he'd have no

compunction about taking her right here and now. Right on the front porch.

Instead, the impending wedding and his own dishonesty kept him from having her at all.

If thoughts like those kept rolling through his head, Reed would not be looking forward to his wedding night.

Chapter Seven

"I still can't believe you're marrying one of the Quarrels boys!" Tucker Dale growled.

Alcina closed her eyes and groaned.

Couldn't her father simply congratulate her and give her his best wishes?

She hoped she wouldn't regret requesting this chat with him in her bedroom while she was trying to finish getting ready herself, but he'd left her with no choice. They needed to get a few things clear between them, and he'd just arrived barely a half hour before the ceremony was to begin.

"Reed is a man, Daddy. A good man." Alcina sat before the mirror, finishing her makeup. A swipe of color over her cheeks with a brush and a light gloss on her lips and she was done. "I remember you always liked Reed."

"It's his father who's the problem."

Remembering they'd once been best friends, she said, "Emmett Quarrels is ill, you know. As a matter of fact, his heart could fail at any time."

"What? Where did you get that idea?"

Alcina faced her father. He appeared as shocked and appalled as he sounded. A good start.

"Everyone in Silver Springs knows. That's why he called his sons home and set up that family corporation. Reed and his brothers are very edgy, because of their father…and because of a lot of bad luck going around the ranch."

She hadn't told him about the fire and her part in saving the horses. Some things were better left unspoken where parents who tended to worry too much were involved.

"The Curly-Q's got bigger problems than simple bad luck," Tucker muttered. "The mortgage is more than two years in arrears and I can't carry Emmett any—"

"Please, Daddy."

So her father *was* considering foreclosure, Alcina realized. She'd been afraid of that. But maybe she could delay things until Reed could reconnoiter. She had the utmost faith in him. He knew what he was doing. He'd been running a bigger spread than the Curly-Q for the past several years. All he needed was time and the ranch would be in the black once more. She would try to buy him that time, but she didn't want to ruin her wedding day with arguments.

Keeping her voice calm, she remained reasonable. "They don't need anything to compound their problems right now. I know I don't."

"All right. This is your wedding day. Any unpleasant discussions can keep a while longer."

She stared at the man who'd raised her with nothing but kindness and respect, a man who still reeked with authority, though he was far past his prime. Unlike Emmett, who had the demeanor of an old and ailing man, Tucker Dale was in good health, fit and trim, silver-haired and handsome. His finely tailored gray suit was the exact shade of his eyes. She'd always known her father to be vain and a bit arrogant, but he'd also always been a good man and a better father, totally supportive of her needs.

"Daddy, promise me something."

"Anything that's in my power to grant is yours, you know that."

"Keep the peace with Emmett, no matter what."

"I won't be starting anything."

"Well, don't finish anything either, okay?" Alcina turned back to the mirror to fuss with wisps of curls that didn't need fussing. "I want my marriage to start on the right foot. I want to make *this* marriage work, Daddy." She wanted Reed to love her and surround her with the large family she'd longed for while growing up. "I want to make sure this lasts forever."

He came up behind her and placed his hands on her shoulders. "Then that's what I want for you, too, darling."

Watching him via the mirror, she said, "My situation is already…complicated. And fragile."

"Complicated how?"

"I haven't told Reed about Jeffrey…and now I just can't."

And she would never admit to her father that she'd accepted Reed's proposal in the form of a business partnership.

"Alcina, do you think that's wise?" he asked reasonably. "Reed is bound to find out."

"Right, because I intend to tell him…sometime." Alcina had convinced herself of that. Once she felt secure in her relationship, she could tell her husband all. "No one here but you and Pru know."

"I think you're making a mistake."

"There's no time!" She wouldn't have Reed calling the marriage off, not before she had a chance at him. "I'm hoping that my husband and I will form the kind of relationship where I can find a way to tell him later…and he'll find a way to understand."

Her father clucked under his breath but didn't rail on as Alcina feared he might. Even so, tension made her fingers clumsy as she donned her single strand of pearls.

"All right," her father finally said, giving her shoulders a comforting squeeze. "I promise I'll do my best to hold my temper in check no matter what that old buzzard Emmett Quarrels says to me."

Alcina sighed in relief. "Thanks, Daddy."

"I'd better let you finish up here. Shall I tell Pru to come back in?"

"Please." Her gaze fell on the small carved and gilded music box perched to one side of her makeup tray. "Wait a minute. Before you go, I need to ask a favor."

"Another one, you mean?"

"Don't worry, this one's not a big deal." She swiveled on her stool to face him. "Someone lost a diamond at Pru and Chance's wedding. I'm holding on to it until that person comes forward to claim it. But it makes me nervous to keep it in the house." The only bank in town had closed when her father had moved his business to Taos a dozen years before. "I thought maybe you could keep the diamond in one of your safe-deposit boxes."

"Of course. In the meantime, you've put it someplace prudent, I hope."

"As secure as it can be right here in plain sight."

Alcina picked up the music box and lifted the lid.

As the mechanism tinkled an old tune, she fingered a catch that could only be pressed in once the lid had been opened. A cleverly secreted drawer slid out from the design on the back. Nested in the dark velvet-lined resting space, the facets of the trillion caught the light to stunning effect.

"Good Lord," Tucker murmured.

He lifted the diamond for a closer look.

Watching her father inspect the stone, Alcina noted that his eyes widened for a moment and his hand shook slightly. Then he cleared his throat, replaced the stone in its velvet setting and stepped back.

"Very unusual," he said, turning from her and moving toward the door. "And quite valuable, I'm sure. You're right to want it in a safe. I'll take the stone with me when I leave."

"Thanks, Daddy."

He threw a kiss her way and exited.

The weather suddenly caught Alcina's attention. Rising, she crossed to the windows. A cold front had come through the night before, and now the afternoon sky was nearly white with big, wet flakes. A light blanket already coated the street below. She wondered how it was that nature could so disguise ugliness— the abandoned buildings scattered here and there along Main Street—and make everything look so picturesque.

Rain was a bad omen for a wedding day. She decided that snow must be a good omen.

Not that she was superstitious.

Alcina slipped out of her silk wrap and was removing her dress from the gown bag when she heard movement outside the bedroom door.

The wedding plans were simple—a short ceremony

in the parlor and a high tea to celebrate. Pru and Josie had helped her make the scones and pastries and finger sandwiches early that morning. They'd warned the men to eat a hearty lunch if they didn't want to starve. Alcina only hoped the men had taken that advice to heart.

Though she had a special late-night meal planned for her and Reed...and the plans for in between were even more special.

"I'm ba-a-ack," Pru called as she whirled through the door.

"Just in time," Alcina said, removing the cream-colored silk dress from its hanger.

Pru helped her into the designer garment, zipped it and secured the two tiny fabric-covered buttons at the top. The dress was a case in slim sophistication with long tight sleeves and an asymmetrical neckline and asymmetrical calf-length hemline. Though Alcina had bought the dress before leaving New York, she'd never had the chance to show it off.

Now she twirled before the mirror, checking her reflection from different angles.

"Reed's eyes are going to pop right out of his head when he sees you in that," Pru said.

"You don't think he'll be disappointed that I didn't go the traditional route?"

"Are you kidding? *This* is you, Alcina. I can't imagine you disappointing any man in that dress. As a matter of fact," Pru teased, "I wouldn't be surprised if your groom falls madly in love today."

"From your lips..."

Pru handed Alcina the small bouquet of cream and yellow roses that she'd fetched from the refrigerator. Remembering that Reed had set a flower in her hair, she pulled a yellow rose from the bunch and worked it into the twisted strands in back.

"Perfect," Pru murmured.

Indeed, Reed appeared to be dazzled when, Pru having preceded her, Alcina stood on the landing of the staircase, alone, sans father. Her having Daddy give her away a second time would be hypocritical…though she really didn't want to dwell on anything having to do with her first and disastrous marriage today.

Obviously entranced with her appearance, Reed moved forward to watch her slowly descend the stairs.

Gathered in the parlor chatting, the guests hushed as if they sensed the moment. Josie and Bart and his two kids, Pru and Chance, Emmett and Felice, Daddy, the Reverend and Mrs. Prescott—all eyes turned toward them.

Reed took three steps up and held out his hand for her. Alcina placed her fingers in his palm and he quickly surrounded them, giving her a quick squeeze of reassurance. Thrilled by the gesture that Alcina felt went beyond business, she was delighted to let him guide her down to the foyer.

"I didn't think you could be more beautiful," Reed said softly. "I was wrong."

Pulse racing, she murmured, "And I didn't think you could be more handsome."

Beneath his black western suit, his white-on-white embroidered shirt was buttoned up to the throat, where a beautiful piece of rose and sage jasper clasped his string tie. A fancy silver buckle decorated his hand-worked leather belt, and he wore a watch whose thick silver band carried the same design.

Sharply parted and slicked back, his reddish-brown hair complemented the pleasing symmetry of his face.

Robert Redford had nothing on him today, Alcina thought as her stomach fluttered alarmingly.

Reed led her to the parlor, the rose and cream wallpaper glowing with natural light reflected from the snow outside the windows.

Pru had bought and set up the flowers as a special wedding present, and she'd gone all out, waiting until Alcina had been upstairs in her bath to assemble them. Different-size vases and pots and baskets of blossoms sat on every available surface. The flowers' sweet scent mingled with that of the cedar burning in the fireplace.

A setting she would never forget, Alcina thought, a little light-headed with pleasure and anticipation.

"Please, everyone, sit," she said, already loving her wedding before the ceremony had even begun.

For she'd restored and furnished both parlor and dining room herself. A special place for a special event. She didn't think she could have chosen a more memorable locale, no matter how long she might have had to plan.

Reed hooked a hand behind her arm and drew her forward, closer to the blazing fire. The only people who remained standing other than the two of them were the Reverend Prescott and their witnesses, Pru and Chance.

As unconventional as the rest of her plans might be, the words of the ceremony remained timeless.

And when Reed promised to honor, protect and cherish her, to endow her with all his worldly goods, he sounded so sincere that Alcina couldn't help but believe that, given time, they would build something deep and true together.

Reed might not be in love with her—yet—but she knew fascination when she saw it. He couldn't take his gaze from her face, not even when his brother Chance handed him the ring and Reed slipped the thick gold wedding band onto her finger. Nor when her best friend gave her his ring and Alcina finished the ritual, officially accepting him as her husband.

"I pronounce you man and wife," Reverend Prescott said. "You may kiss the bride."

Alcina's heart thundered as Reed slipped his hands around her waist and tugged until she was flat against him. Eyes wide, she noted the tilt of his head, the suggestive sparkle in his eyes, the grin that parted his mouth, which then disappeared from view as it settled over hers.

She opened to him, her acceptance a promise of things to come. Heat flared in her middle and quickly spread to her extremities, and she feared they were too near the fireplace, that she might go up in a blaze so bright that she would simply burn out and vanish.

Reed held her tighter and deepened the kiss.

Until the catcalls began.

Oohs and aahs.

A whistle.

A childish snicker.

Increasingly aware of their audience, they broke apart, the kiss over too fast for Alcina to savor properly. She felt a flush creep up her neck and noted that Reed's complexion seemed a bit high, as well.

Then the guests were out of their seats, surrounding the newlyweds, hugging and kissing the bride, shaking the groom's hand and slapping him on the back, congratulating him on his good sense for marrying her.

When Alcina glanced at her new husband—*she could hardly believe it*—he seemed to be beaming with the same happiness she was feeling.

Finally, her father enveloped her in a bear hug, kissed her forehead and admonished Reed, "You see that my daughter is happy or else."

Reed's smile tightened and Alcina's pulse began to thread unevenly.

But when he said, "I'll do my best to honor her as she deserves," emotion flooded her.

"If you don't," Emmett said, moving in on them while ignoring his old partner, "you'll have a lot to answer for."

Alcina felt a strange vibration between father and son, and Reed's smile died altogether.

What had just happened?

Emmett got between her and her father, threw his arms around her and kissed her cheek. "You're a Quarrels now, girl, just you remember that. Nothing more important than family loyalty and keeping the spread out of—"

"Pa!"

Alcina started at Reed's near shout.

The old man grumbled and coughed and avoided looking at his son or at her.

The strained silence was short-lived, however. Felice saw to that. She marched up to her employer and took his arm.

"Mr. Emmett, perhaps you should sit down until the refreshments are served," she firmly suggested.

"All right. You don't have to pull on me."

Alcina raised her eyebrows at how docile Emmett

became under Felice's direction, and she suddenly wondered if there was more than an employer-employee relationship between them. Felice had worked forever for the man who'd been deemed impossible to live with both by three wives and three sons.

"I've already put on the kettle," Josie announced, coming through the swinging door between kitchen and dining area. She set a tray of finger sandwiches they'd made that morning on the buffet. "Pru and I will take over in the kitchen. We'll be set with refreshments in about ten minutes."

"If you can call them little sandwiches eating," Emmett grumbled.

"Ten minutes is long enough for me to take some photos," Lainey announced.

As they obliged his niece, Alcina sensed the shift in Reed's humor. He was less relaxed around her. Tight even, almost as if he was angry about something. Not that she could fathom his change of mood.

And when he kissed her again, this time it was merely for the camera. None of the delicious heat she'd experienced at the end of the ceremony.

Disappointed, not understanding what had gone sour, Alcina felt her spirits sink. And by the time Josie called them to the buffet, she had no appetite at all.

Still, Alcina went through the motions, using an antique silver utensil to transfer the finger sandwiches—roast beef, salmon, egg salad and olive-pecan, which stood in place of the impossible-to-buy watercress. She added a warm scone, strawberry jam and cream to her plate.

Different varieties of loose tea leaves steeped in

three fancy silver serving pots Alcina had bought over the years. She poured herself a cup of Earl Grey.

Sitting at one end of the table adorned in layers of silk and lace and velvet, set with fine china and crystal and silver, Alcina fidgeted. Opposite her new husband, who now appeared a bit down-at-the-mouth, she chafed to be alone with him, to have a private discussion, to find out what in the world was bothering him.

She wasn't left to her thoughts for long, however. The table soon filled. Crowded together as they were, the happy guests became rowdy, everyone seemingly talking at once. Not exactly the picture of any formal high tea she'd attended in the past, Alcina thought.

But nice.

She found herself relaxing.

"Eeow, this stuff's weird!" Lainey suddenly said, dropping half a finger sandwich to her plate.

Olive-pecan, Alcina noted, lips quivering into a smile as everyone laughed.

"So you two get married and we get to go on the honeymoon," Chance said. "Remember we're leaving for the National Rodeo Finals early Tuesday morning."

Where he would compete in the saddle bronc and bareback competitions, Alcina knew.

"What about you, Josie?" Pru asked. "Have you decided to compete?"

Josie barrel raced a flaxen-maned sorrel that she had hand-raised. Despite her having only entered a couple of rodeos since arriving in Silver Springs, she'd previously earned enough winnings to be in the top fifteen contestants in the country, so she, too, was eligible for the National.

"I'm in."

"Which means you'll be shorthanded, Barton," Emmett muttered.

"Actually, I might not be around, either," Bart said. "I got a call this morning from the real estate agent handling the house. Seems that finally we have a serious buyer. If the contract and financing can be worked out fast enough, I may be taking the kids into Albuquerque for a few days, as well."

"I can see my friends?" Lainey asked excitedly. "Yay!"

"If you *had* any friends," Daniel said.

Lainey threatened to poke him with her fork until Felice clucked at her.

Only Emmett was obviously unhappy. "What are we going to do without you around the spread for days on end?"

"I think I can manage, Pa," Reed said dryly. "I have a little experience running a ranch, if you remember."

"Of course you do, Son," Emmett mumbled. "I don't know what I was thinking." He was looking at Alcina when he said, "So you'll be staying at the house while Bart and my grandkids are gone."

Startled by the suggestion, Alcina said, "I have a house right here."

"But you're going to be moving to the ranch eventually. We'll add a wing to the house and—"

"Pa, whoa!" Reed said. "Hold on. Where we live is between Alcina and me. We haven't had any time to make firm plans for the future."

"The Curly-Q *is* your future!" Emmett insisted, coughing. And then with a wheeze he added, "And the future of the kids you're gonna have."

Emmett turned his stare toward Alcina's father when he made that particular announcement.

Mortifying Alcina.

She and Reed hadn't even talked about living arrangements…or children…or anything!

"We haven't made a toast yet," Felice suddenly said as if to undercut the growing tension. "Who can open the champagne?"

"I believe that's the best man's job," Chance said, rising.

On the buffet, three bottles awaited in a silver champagne bucket.

The conversation went more smoothly from there, but Alcina felt a renewal of the edge between Reed and Emmett. At least her father had kept his promise to keep the peace. She sensed he'd wanted to say something strident to Emmett more than once. Instead, he'd said nothing at all.

Thankful for that, she smiled at him, and he smiled at her in return.

Alcina sighed. Maybe all the tension at the table was in her own head, she thought, her own guilt casting shadows where there were none.

Meeting her husband's steady, serious gaze comforted her. Everything would be all right.

It had to be.

REED WASN'T CERTAIN how he managed to get through his own wedding party. The ceremony had gone well enough, but immediately afterward, Pa had managed to set him on edge. For one heart-stopping moment, he'd thought the old man was going to face down Tucker about the mortgage right there in the midst of the celebration.

Thank God for Felice.

Now the guests had gone, all but Tucker. Even Josie had vacated her room for the night—Bart's woman was bunking in with Lainey to give them a night of complete privacy.

As the time for him to be alone with his new wife approached, Reed was experiencing a different kind of tension, one he couldn't quite delineate. It wasn't as if he hadn't had his share of women, after all.

"Daddy, you can't drive home," Alcina protested when Tucker tried to get his coat from the hall closet. "Not on those roads in this snow. There's no rush for you to get back to Taos, anyway. And we have plenty of rooms available, as you well know."

"But this is your first night together as man and wife," Tucker protested. "I don't want to impose."

"You're not imposing. You're family. I expect you to stay. So does Reed. Right, Reed?"

"Yes, of course."

There went the complete privacy, but how could he argue with her logic?

"All right, sweetheart, anything you say."

"Good. Then let me show you to your room and make sure you have everything you need. And if you're hungry, I can zap something in the microwave and bring it up to you."

"That's very thoughtful," Tucker said. "I could use some food with a little substance."

Reed watched father and daughter ascend the stairs, arm-in-arm. Alcina glanced back once and made a what-else-was-I-supposed-to-do face at him.

So they wouldn't be alone, after all, Reed thought. Great. As if he didn't have enough to strangle his gut as it was.

His motive for asking Alcina to marry him in the first place hadn't been pure, a fact that had been eating away at him all week, even though he'd put it to her as a business deal. That still wasn't totally honest, which she deserved. She would never have accepted if she'd known he'd only asked in an attempt to save the ranch through leverage with her father. And he'd done so at Pa's suggestion. He feared he was more like Pa than he wanted to admit.

And the business part bothered him, anyway. It didn't seem like business to him when he'd held Alcina in his arms. Kissing her had been very, very personal...as was what would happen between them once she got her father settled in.

He'd been awake most of the previous night.

Thinking about holding Alcina in his arms...undressing her...exploring her lush body to his heart's content. The imagining had made him hard with raw hunger for her. He'd wanted to make her moan...make her beg for more...make her cry out in completion.

And now they wouldn't even be alone.

Unable to relax, Reed paced the length of the parlor, trying to determine the best way to approach the awkward situation. He hadn't considered having to discuss anything with Alcina.

A drink in front of the fire...one kiss leading to another...her rubbing against him like a cat in heat...him carrying her up the staircase to the bedroom...

That's how he'd imagined it would happen.

"Reed?" Alcina called from the top of the staircase. "Are you all right?"

He turned to look at her, even more stunning than

she'd been a couple of hours before when he'd married her. If that were possible.

"I'm just thinking," he said. "Trying to shake the tension of the big day."

She descended quickly but kept some distance between them. "What's wrong? It's Daddy, isn't it? Should I have sent him on his way?"

"No, you were right about the weather."

Suddenly the moment was here and he was struck dumb. He had to say something to get the ball rolling. Sweat trickled between his shoulder blades and down his back. He felt as impotent as he had so many times with his father and brother, when he'd wanted to assert himself but just couldn't.

Reed told himself not to panic...that logic had worked with the marriage proposal...

"Don't worry," he said, "I won't let your father's presence interfere with my...uh...my husbandly duties."

She laughed. "Your what?"

Her expression made him cringe inside. He'd been getting himself tied in a knot and she was amused.

"I know we both think of this marriage as a kind of business deal, but—"

"But what?" she asked, her amusement vanishing. "Are you saying that you're willing to put yourself out to seal the deal, so to speak?"

Hell, he'd gone and said the exact wrong thing. He'd never been good with fancy words. He was better at doing. Stepping toward Alcina, he slipped his arms around her back and brushed her lips with his. At least she didn't turn away her head.

"You're my wife now," he said simply. "And we both have our...physical needs."

Stiffening, she flattened her hands on his chest and pushed him away. "Well, I can control mine!"

Heat rose along his neck. He wasn't doing too well here. Nor was she.

Her stance reminded him of what she'd been like that first day he'd been home, all prickly and ready to fight at the drop of a hat.

"As long as our marriage is strictly business," Alcina said, her tone unnaturally sweet, "that precludes anything from happening in the bedroom."

An idea that hadn't occurred to him.

"Wait a minute!" he said indignantly. "I thought you wanted to build a life together."

And as far as he was concerned, that life included sex. With her.

"I do want to build a life together," she insisted.

"Then what's the problem?"

"Business partners don't bed each other."

"But we're more than business partners. We're married. We have a certificate that says so."

"A piece of paper means nothing in a relationship!" She crossed her arms over her chest. "Can you honestly say you have any true feelings for me?"

Reed shifted uneasily. He liked Alcina...most of the time. He cared about what happened to her and wanted the best for her. But if she was asking for a declaration of love, he couldn't give that to her. He didn't know her well enough to be in love with her and he wouldn't outright lie about it to get her into bed with him.

Omitting the whole truth about his proposal had been bad enough.

"I can control myself, as well," he muttered.

"That's what I thought." Alcina laughed again, but

this time he heard a definite chill in her tone. "Until your heart is in this marriage—*if* that ever happens— you can sleep in one of the other bedrooms, Reed Quarrels."

"What will your father think?"

"Whatever Daddy thinks doesn't matter. He won't interfere. This is between you and me."

Reed fisted his hands at his sides. "Well, I'd rather not sleep in another bedroom."

"Then sleep anywhere you want, for all I care. But it's not going to be in bed with me!"

"Then it's not going to be in this house!"

"Fine!"

"Fine!"

Reed stormed over to the coat closet and pulled out his leather jacket and Stetson. He wouldn't stay where he wasn't wanted.

And it was obvious that Alcina didn't want him.

She waited until he reached the front door before asking, "Reed, where are you going?"

"Home. To my trailer," he amended, thinking his home should be with her. "We can talk about our situation after we've had time to cool down and discuss this reasonably."

Though Reed was certain that Alcina could be cool to him as long as it suited her.

Chapter Eight

Late that night, unable to sleep or to stand Reed's walking out on her any longer, Alcina dressed for the weather, wrote her father a cheery note so that he wouldn't worry about her and left the house.

She wanted Reed badly enough to go after him, but she'd been serious about requiring his heart be in their relationship before she would share a bed with him. And winning his heart would be difficult to accomplish long distance.

So, deciding to brave the weather that had let up earlier, she dragged an overnight bag out to her car and threw it in the trunk. Then she found her brush and scraper and proceeded to clean off the snow.

She was nearly finished, when a movement nearby caught her by surprise.

Her pulse charged and she stared down a darkened Main Street, where against the moonlit glare of snow, she saw a large silhouette suddenly bolt between two abandoned buildings.

No other movement on the street, not even a vehicle.

No light.

So what had he been doing there?

Watching her? she wondered. Or watching the bed-and-breakfast?

Whomever she'd seen was undoubtedly a transient, she told herself. Just someone passing through town, maybe looking for work or a handout. Nothing to worry about.

But she found herself worrying, anyway.

Her pulse wouldn't settle and her stomach knotted. And when she got behind the wheel, she locked her doors before starting the engine. She fixed her gaze on those abandoned buildings and drove slowly by them.

But her extra caution went unrewarded. She saw nothing to alarm her. Thankfully. Whomever she had seen had simply disappeared.

Breathing a sigh of relief, wondering at her attack of big-city paranoia, she returned her thoughts to her purpose.

Reed's walking out on her had been devastating at first, but she'd gotten over feeling sorry for herself and chose instead to consider herself challenged.

She was going to make her husband fall for her.

Whatever it took…

Like Temporary, she would make him see that he didn't want to be without her. She would lavish him with attention and affection and, if it didn't nauseate her, adoration, to boot. Undoubtedly, both Pru and Josie would have some cogent thoughts on the matter.

She could use all the help she could get.

Once on Curly-Q land, she followed the back road that would take her to Reed. A five-minute drive and she was there. Unfortunately, even the pristine snow and moonlight couldn't make art of the ratty old trailer that Reed called home.

Groaning, Alcina banged her forehead against the steering wheel, but even the pain didn't knock some sense into her. She remained set on her purpose.

Slipping out of the car, she heard barking from inside the trailer. Then the door suddenly opened and Temporary leaped out and rushed her.

Even as she bent to pat the dog, Reed said, "Alcina, what the hell are you doing out here in the middle of the night?"

He was framed in the doorway, barefoot and half-nude. He'd pulled on jeans but hadn't even zipped them all the way. As her mouth went dry, she licked her lips and forced her gaze from the splash of hair revealed below his waist up to his face. He appeared confused. And annoyed. His hair was sleep-tousled around his unusually harsh features.

And her knees were weakening.

Taking a big breath, Alcina drew herself together and pulled a case from the back seat. "I'm moving in with you. We're married, remember?"

"I believe I reminded you of that fact earlier, and you said you didn't intend to sleep with me."

"I still don't. I assume you have a couch."

He groaned and asked, "What's this all about?"

"Appearances," she said, knowing that he had a conscience as big as his heart but far easier to manipulate. "I won't have people sneering at me behind my back because my husband up and left me on our wedding night." When he didn't say anything, she shivered and said, "It's cold out here. Are you going to let me in or not?"

"C'mon."

Reed stood back from the door and Temporary shot through the opening before her.

With a sense of growing irony, Alcina crossed the threshold of her new home on her own two feet.

ENSCONCED COMFORTABLY in his office chair late the next morning, door closed against accidental eavesdroppers, Emmett Quarrels faced down his former partner, who sat on the other side of the desk.

"You've got a lot of nerve, Tuck, coming here after threatening to foreclose on the Curly-Q."

"Emmett, if this weren't your ranch, and if I didn't have a sentimental streak a mile wide, I would have foreclosed long ago," Tucker informed him.

"Sentimental? Hah!"

"I'm a banker, not a social worker. But I respect the past even if we're no longer friends. I'm here to make you an offer you shouldn't refuse."

"What kind of offer?" Emmett asked.

Wouldn't do to sound too interested.

"Assistance so that you can put enough in your bank account to catch up on the mortgage payments." Emmett tried not to show his glee. His plan was already working. The very day after Reed married Alcina, the old goat was ready to open his bank account to ensure his daughter's future.

"What kind of assistance would that be?" he asked, making the question sound gruff and disinterested.

"Help in dividing up your holdings and selling some of them off."

Emmett stalled out on that one. He sat there in shock. Not at all what he'd expected to hear.

He'd never cared for the wealth provided them both by the played-out silver mine. Only the independent life he'd managed to grab onto had ever mattered. The small-town boy with holes in his pockets had turned himself into a land-rich rancher. He'd taught himself what he needed to know to live off his land. And for that, he'd always considered himself wealthy.

"Can't do it," he said tightly. "I incorporated all my holdings into a family deal. Everything is tied together and in the hands of my boys."

"Then talk to them and get Howard Siles in on the deal. Get it all untied!" Tucker told him.

"Why is this so important to you?"

"It's not important to me! It's important to you and your family. You may have a failing ticker, Emmett, but you aren't blind, deaf and dumb, even if you're acting like you are. Unless you do something and fast, you and your boys are going to be looking for a place to live."

Suspicions about his former partner rising anew, Emmett asked, "So what did you have in mind, Tuck?"

"I can put you in touch with a developer who wants to build houses on horse properties for people with too much money in their pockets."

"I'll bet you can," Emmett muttered.

"And he could use some of that property in town, as well," Tucker continued. "People with money expect amenities close at hand. A sparkling new convenience store. A fancy coffee shop. That kind of thing. If you think about it, it's a perfect plan. You would only lose part of the ranch and you could be solvent again, at least for a couple of years."

Familiar words that he'd heard only the week before. From Vernon Martell…

Furious, Emmett wondered if Tucker was in cahoots with the neighboring rancher, who'd made no bones about wanting to get his hands on some of the Curly-Q land. The thing about the horse properties could be nothing more than a cover so that he wouldn't know where the offer was coming from.

Emmett stared at the man who once had been his best friend.

A lifetime ago, he and Tucker and Noah Warner had been young and full of big dreams. After finding a huge new vein of silver, they'd reopened the abandoned silver mine and had worked it until it paid off. Then they'd rebuilt the ailing town. Noah hadn't lasted that far—not a man of vision, he'd preferred gambling to backbreaking labor. He'd let himself be bought out early on, had taken his share of the profit and run.

But Emmett Quarrels and Tucker Dale—by God, they'd been some team!

Until their relationship dried up, just as the mine had.

And when things had gone sour between them, Tucker sold out, returning to a more genteel and profitable life as a banker like his daddy before him. And like his wife Nancy's people, as well, for that matter.

Their parting had not been amicable.

And now Emmett had new doubts about his former partner. "What is it, Tuck? Old age making you live in the past? All these years, you waited for a little revenge."

Tucker put on a good imitation of a man who'd just been insulted. Emmett would give him that.

"It's not my fault that you've gone in arrears on your mortgage payments."

"Isn't it?"

Silence stretched between them. Silence and

Tucker's outraged expression. His features turned blood-red at the accusation.

"What are you saying, Emmett? That you think *I'm* responsible for your bad luck?"

"Maybe there's no such thing as bad luck," Emmett returned. "Maybe everything bad that's happened on the Curly-Q is your fault!"

An idea that had come to him well before the threat of foreclosure. Ever since the bad-luck incidents had started and the telephone calls had begun, Emmett had wondered if his nemesis was behind the scheme.

"You can't seriously believe that of me."

"Why not? You never forgave me because I blew the whistle on your dirty little game. Maybe you've been plotting against me for years, and when I was alone and got sick you saw your chance to move in and bankrupt me like the financial snake you've become."

Tucker rose. "When you've come to your senses, call me. There's something I think you need to see—"

"You're not going nowhere!" Emmett popped out of his seat. "Not until you admit your guilt."

"Are you sure it's not *your* guilt that's bothering you, Emmett?"

"What?" Emmett fisted his hands and set them on the desk as he leaned toward his former partner. "I haven't fabricated the bad luck that's been plaguing us!"

Tucker leaned forward, meeting him eye-to-eye. "Maybe one of your other victims isn't quite so forgiving as I was."

"That's a crock! Besides, you deserved worse than you ever got!"

"You couldn't make a woman happy, so when Sunny turned to me just to find out what she was doing wrong, you jumped to conclusions and made sure Nancy heard your garbage about Sunny and me being lovers."

Plagued by his third wife's desertion, Emmett was near to seeing red. "At least Nancy stuck by you."

"In body, perhaps, but not in spirit. She stayed with me for Alcina and Charles, and once they went away to school, she felt free to leave, as well. You made it impossible for me to have my own wife...or to find a woman to replace her. And all because you drove Chance's mother off the ranch and then you let him believe she abandoned him!"

Unable to take any more, Emmett yelled, "That's a damn lie!" and hurled himself up and over the desk at his nemesis. Even as the two men went flying backward into the chair, he heard a buzzing in his ears.

"Pa!" Reed yelled. "What the hell do you think you're doing?"

But Emmett's fists were flying and connecting, and he was taking his share of punches in return. He hadn't felt this good in years.

Suddenly, he was lifted off Tucker by the scruff of his neck, his shirt nearly strangling him in the process. He lashed out ineffectually, Reed merely dancing out of the way.

"I don't believe it, Pa!" Reed yelled. "Look at you, practically foaming at the mouth to get into a brawl...and you're hardly out of breath. Great calisthenics, Pa, for a man who's *supposed to be dying!*"

Emmett cursed a blue streak.

The jig was up.

ALCINA WAS OFF for her bed-and-breakfast about an hour after Reed headed for the ranch house to report to work. She'd needed to shower and do something with her makeup and hair, and the tiny bathroom in the trailer fought her every inch of the way. Nevertheless, she had her standards, so she did the best she could.

Too bad Reed hadn't stuck around to see her after she'd taken care of the bird's nest her hair had become without her satin-covered pillow. No matter that they'd been married the day before and that everyone would have understood if he hadn't shown for work at all, he'd jumped into his clothes and whipped out of the trailer before she'd even had time to protest.

Sighing, Alcina figured he'd been relieved to be able to get away from her.

Just as she was relieved to be able to get out of the trailer that gave her claustrophobia. And one night in that rotten little bed and she already needed her Jacuzzi for her aching back muscles. But as badly as she'd fared, it had been worse for Reed, she thought with a grin.

He'd slept on the couch that had been a full six inches too short for him.

At his own insistence, of course.

Always the gentleman. She'd give him that.

Hoping to see her father in person before he left for Taos, Alcina was disappointed to find his car gone. Well, what had she expected, he wouldn't know she would be back this early and the weather had sure cleared.

Sometime during the early-morning hours, a warm front had chased away the cold, and the white blanket that had settled over the ground the night before had already gone patchy. By midafternoon, when temperatures would reach the high fifties according to the local weatherman, there would be no sign of snow, she knew.

For some reason, Alcina hesitated entering the empty house. She wanted to hear voices. Conversation. Laughter. Reed had withheld those from her. After she'd stormed his domain, he'd withdrawn into one of his quiet, thoughtful moods.

Maybe a visit to Pru was in order. Her friend could cheer her up and give her tips on how to win over her very own Quarrels boy, as Daddy had called Reed.

But first she had to attend to Miss Kitty as she'd promised Josie when she'd volunteered to vacate the premises for the night. The cat needed fresh food and water, not to mention a warm word and a pat on the head.

Alcina needed that, too, but Reed hadn't seen fit to give it to her this morning.

Leaving the car on the street in front, Alcina circled the building and entered the house via the mudroom.

"Miss Kitty!" she sang out, expecting to be assaulted by one hungry cat.

But the house was oddly still and Alcina only had to take one step inside the kitchen to realize why.

Cabinet doors and drawers stood open, their contents strewn every which way. Canisters had been dumped, their contents littering the counters.

Breath caught in her throat, pulse thundering through the rest of her, Alcina could hardly grasp that someone had wreaked such havoc on her place.

And could still be here...

Cautiously, she backed off, feeling her way into the

mudroom, eyes glued to the swinging door that led to the front of the house. Intent, she didn't sense another presence until she smacked into the body behind her.

Jerking and screaming, Alcina flew around, fists flailing at the intruder.

"Wow!" Wide-eyed and ashen, Josie jumped back fast. "What in the world's going on?"

Alcina sagged. "Th-the kitchen. Look."

Josie poked her head through the doorway. "Oh, Lord."

"I thought you were the intruder. Let's get out of here, go get help."

"Bart's tied up with family business right now— Reed, too. That's why I came back to check on Miss Kitty. Where is she?"

Alcina shook her head.

"I'll be right back."

Before Alcina could stop her, Josie shot out the door. No way did she want to be in the house alone, so Alcina followed. But Josie only went as far as the back of the ranch pickup she'd driven. There she grabbed a rifle from the rack and checked to make certain it was loaded.

Alcina hated guns. Eyeing the rifle that Josie handled so expertly, she said, "You want to go back in there without someone checking the place out first?"

Josie moved back toward the entry, muttering, "We don't exactly have a lawman around unless you count Bart and, like I said, he's unavailable right now. My cat's in there, so I'm doing the checking."

"Not alone," Alcina muttered.

Whipping through the mudroom, she picked up a broom with a thick wooden shaft. Not exactly a true weapon, but it would do some serious damage. Besides, it made her feel better holding on to something solid.

She and Josie went through the house together, side by side, checking each room carefully for some other presence before moving on to the next. Alcina was distraught at the mess, especially at Pru's flowers, dumped and strewn all over, crushed under some uncaring boot heel.

"I don't understand why some would-be thief would do this," Alcina murmured, half in shock.

"Frustration," Josie said, keeping alert, sweeping her gaze beyond the room and holding her rifle at the ready. "The guy's obviously a loser. What he did here has nothing to do with you personally."

But Alcina couldn't rid herself of the horrible suspicion that it *was* personal. That someone could hate her, and her not even be aware of it, gave her the creeps.

That creepy feeling stayed with her as she and Josie climbed the staircase together.

An unexpected crash from somewhere upstairs made her heart lurch.

Alcina clutched Josie's arm and whispered, "Maybe this is a bad idea."

But her friend's expression was determined. "No one will ever make me run away again."

Alcina sighed. There were two of them and Josie was armed. They'd be all right.

Nevertheless, her breath came ragged as they took the last few stairs and began to check the bedrooms. Objects she'd bought with love had been treated with the utmost disrespect and were strewn everywhere.

Alcina swallowed her upset, refused to let it work

against her. She needed to harness her own anger to stay safe.

In silence, they went through one bedroom at a time, ever on the alert for some intruder waiting in the shadows for his chance to jump out at them. They eliminated one room after the other and paused when they got to the last—Josie's.

They stared at each other. Alcina took a deep breath, licked her lips and nodded.

They burst through the door as one...this room, too, was empty.

Relief had barely washed through Alcina when a thunk in the closet made her go tight once more. The door was cracked open.

Josie took a stance, rifle raised and aimed.

And gripping the broom in her right hand, Alcina stood back and reached for the doorknob with her left. She snatched the door open so fast she stumbled backward...

And the cat came flying out at them, yowling indignantly.

Both women started, then sagged with relief.

"Oh, Lord, it's just the cat," Alcina said shakily. "Whoever was here is gone."

"Come here, you," Josie cooed.

She set down the rifle to gather the frightened animal into her arms. Miss Kitty clung to her pitifully and complained in her own cat fashion.

"So what went on here?" Josie asked.

Alcina shook her head. Knees weak, she lowered herself to Josie's bed. "I—I guess I've been robbed."

"But of what? The silver was still on the buffet. Wouldn't a thief have taken that?"

"Maybe the pattern wasn't to his taste?" Alcina

said, laughing and hiccuping at the same time. "Maybe he was just looking for cash."

Rising suddenly, she headed for her own room, a mess equal to the others. It took her only a minute to check for her stash, which she kept along with her checkbook in the top drawer of the chest.

"That's it. I had nearly three hundred dollars here. It's gone. He got what he wanted."

Relieved, she decided Josie had been right, the intruder's wreckage hadn't been personal. He'd just been frustrated looking for the cash.

"But who?"

"Last night, when I left for Reed's trailer, I saw someone up the street. I thought maybe he was watching the house, but then he disappeared. Thank God he didn't break in while Daddy was here alone."

Then she saw it, the music box, lying on its side on the floor next to the dresser.

"He probably didn't want to hurt anyone, just wanted some money," Josie said. "How good of a look did you get?"

"Not good." Alcina picked up the treasure. "Too dark. All I saw was his shape. Big." Tightening her grip on the music box, she concentrated. "I keep thinking there's something else…I just can't put my finger on it. He's probably a transient and long gone back to the highway."

"Let's hope you're right."

The music box…

Alcina lifted the lid, and when the tune began playing, she triggered the catch that released the secret, velvet-lined drawer.

Empty!

"PA'S A FRAUD," Reed announced to his brothers once he assembled the family meeting in the living room nearly an hour later.

Tucker had finally left.

The two old men had turned on him, had told him to butt out and had sent him packing. They'd had some unfinished business, according to Tucker, and in disgust, Reed had left them to it and to their raised voices. And to their raised fists, for all he knew or cared.

Well, Pa was finished now.

"Pa's not dying," Reed announced to all. "As a matter of fact, he's healthy as a mule."

"Not quite," the old man said. "I may not be on my deathbed, but I do have a bad ticker!"

Felice cleared her throat and gave him a look.

Which Pa ignored.

"I had a real scare last year about the time Sara was killed," he said of Bart's late wife. "Thought it was a heart attack. That's why I wasn't at the funeral. I landed in the hospital for a few days for all them tests."

"Felice?" Bart said, looking to her for confirmation.

"That part is true, Mr. Reed," she said. "But Dr. Baxter said that if Mr. Emmett took his medicine, changed his diet and modified his activities, he could live to be ninety. I apologize deeply that I let him talk me into keeping my silence."

Pa at ninety, nothing would make Reed happier. But right at the moment he was damn angry with the old man! Pa had been using everyone, especially him.

"So nothing's changed," Bart said, shaking his head.

Chance gave their father a look of disgust. "You've been manipulating us all."

"Now wait a minute. I had good reason. That scare made me realize what's important in life. Family. I wanted my sons home, where they've always belonged. I wanted to get to know my grandkids. All of them," he said pointedly, staring at Chance. "I figured if I just asked you all, you wouldn't come."

"And the bad-luck incidents had nothing to do with it, I suppose," Reed said.

Clever as always, Pa talked around the direct question. "This ranch has always been your legacy. I didn't think you'd want to see it disappear."

"You could have been honest, Pa," Reed said, "for once in your life."

"I knew this wasn't going to work," Chance said, sounding disappointed.

"What are you talking about?" Emmett demanded. "It *has* been working. We're all pulling together and—"

"No, you're pulling the strings again," Chance said. "Bart never wanted to be a rancher. The law's his life. You guilted him into doing what you wanted."

"That's not totally true," Bart said. "I wanted to get my kids away from the city gangs. I was glad for the excuse to come back where I could give them a better life."

"Are you saying you preferred the responsibility of this ranch to your career in law enforcement?" When Bart said nothing, Chance grunted. "Thought so. And what about Reed? He's the one with the fire for ranching. And the experience. He should be running this place."

All eyes turned to Reed. This was his moment, he knew. He should speak out and now. Chance was nothing if not perceptive. But the moment of opportunity passed too quickly before he could speak, and his little brother went on.

"And what about me, Pa?" Chance asked. "You won't even discuss my rodeo school. Or the other ideas I have about bringing in money to the spread through tourists. But a rodeo school would involve kids and cowboys from ranches all around. And it sure would be a start in the right direction to help keep this place in the black. Maybe when I get to the National, I ought to ask around, see if someone else is interested. Pru might not like leaving Silver Springs, but she's already told me she'll follow me anywhere."

"And maybe I'd better rethink my job situation," Bart said. "Sheriff Olvera called last week and said that I had to be back at work by the first of the year or my job is gone forever. Maybe I need to rethink selling our house in Albuquerque."

Trying not to panic, Reed said, "Whoa, not so fast. Just because Pa tricked us is no reason to give up. He backed himself into a corner. Legally. Any decisions about the direction of the ranch or who does what is up to us, not him." Above all, Reed feared that his brothers would give up and sell out just as Pa had predicted. "And now that we know he's not dying, we don't have to pussyfoot around him just to make him happy."

He was certain the family-corporation ranch could work. It was what he'd always wanted—him and Chance and Bart working toward a common goal— with him heading it up, of course. Not that he'd ever put that to words. He might have swallowed his own youthful expectations, but he'd never forgotten them.

Hell, no, he didn't want to quit.

Besides which, now he was saddled with a wife that Pa had tricked him into marrying. One that he didn't know how to handle. He was already aware of what Alcina thought about his trailer. Not that she had said much. No way would she go off to live with him in it only God knew where so that he could work another man's spread.

They could get an annulment, since the marriage hadn't been consummated.

But he just couldn't do it.

Maybe his heart was creeping in the right direction, after all, Reed thought, not without a bit of irony.

Or maybe it was that, in addition to being fond of Alcina and admiring her, Reed wanted the marriage to work if for no other reason than to prove that one could for a Quarrels man despite Pa's terrible record.

After all, he was nothing like Pa...

Reed winced at the denial. He'd helped Pa by keeping the whole truth from his brothers from the moment he'd known it. And more important, from Alcina.

As long as all this honesty was going on, she would have to know everything, as well. Including the reason he'd proposed in the first place. And she would have to know soon. Then she might file for the annulment, Reed thought, wondering why the notion was so depressing.

Reed turned his focus back to the family meeting.

"Pa, it's time you showed Chance and Bart that warning you've been keeping from them."

"What warning?" Bart demanded.

Felice fetched the cigar box and Pa pulled out the missive and handed it to Bart.

Both he and Chance were ticked to high heaven after reading the contents and hearing about the myriad calls from real estate agents following every bad-luck incident on the ranch.

"This means someone is trying to ruin the Curly-Q to force you to sell," Bart said. "We're talking felony. Why the hell haven't you gotten the sheriff's department on this?"

"No proof," Emmett said.

"Why didn't you tell me, then?"

"You were trying to get your kids away from one kind of crime," Emmett said. "I didn't think you would be willing to pull them into the middle of another."

Bart swore a blue streak even as the front door flew open and Alcina burst into the house followed by Josie. Both women looked a bit strange.

"Alcina," Reed said. "Is something wrong?"

"Something's wrong, all right." Her eyes welled up and she appeared ready to cry. "I've been robbed!"

Chapter Nine

Alcina was fighting uncharacteristic tears when Reed strode to her and wrapped his arms around her.

"Thank God you're all right." He grasped her by the shoulders and pushed her away to look deep into her eyes. "You are all right, aren't you? You weren't hurt?"

"I wasn't mugged," she said. "It was the bed-and-breakfast. The place is in a shambles. The thief got about three hundred dollars. Thank God Daddy was already gone. I mean, I assume so, because his car wasn't there. But I'm getting worried because I've tried calling him at home a couple of times and the machine answers."

"That's because he was here until a little while ago," Reed said.

"Here?" She looked around, realizing for the first time that she wasn't the only one who was stressed. "Sorry. I didn't mean to interrupt business."

"You're more important than business any day."

"Really?"

"Really."

Alcina couldn't help herself. She threw her arms around Reed's waist and wept. Reed tightened his hold on her. And she felt a hand steal up her back. His fingers caressed the soft flesh of her neck.

In a moment, she shuddered and whispered, "I'm all right, really," as she lifted her head.

"We're done here for now," Bart said, rising from his chair. "We've got some big thinking to do. We can continue the discussion later."

Alcina sniffed and Reed dragged from his pocket a big linen handkerchief. Cupping her chin, he tilted her face and dabbed under both eyes.

"Mascara's running," he said. "You look a little like a raccoon."

She frowned up at him. "But I wear water-proof...okay, you're teasing me, right?"

"Trying to put a smile back on that lovely face," he murmured.

His low whiskey tone sent shocks through her system. As did the fact that he was trying to make her feel better after she'd put him through the hell of a too-short couch and celibate wedding night.

Emmett moved out of the room, his head turned away from her, making Alcina wonder what that was about. He was carrying a cigar box, mumbling to himself. She caught something about partners selling out...

"Ahem!" Bart cleared his throat. "Maybe we'd better get over to the bed-and-breakfast to take a look."

Alcina nodded. "I would appreciate that."

"I'll drive your car," Reed told her.

For once she found no reason to argue with him. She even let him open the passenger door for her and close it after she slid inside.

On the other side of the yard, Bart and Chance and Josie all climbed into Chance's shiny blue pickup.

Reed waited until they were on the road to ask, "So the money is all that was missing, right?"

"I think so. I didn't take inventory. Then there's the diamond, but Daddy probably has that. I won't know until I can talk to him."

"What diamond?"

"The one Reba found at the fire."

"Yeah, I heard something about that. She was looking for the owner, right?"

"Right. Well, she gave it to me to give to Pru, only Pru didn't want to be responsible because it's so valuable and the kids are into everything—"

"So when did Reba give it to you?"

"On the day she died," Alcina said with a shiver. Sighing, she laid her head back against the seat, thankful that Reed didn't ply her with more questions.

The way the brothers responded to her crisis made her feel warm inside. They were all working together to resolve what had happened to her, just like a real family.

After doing a walk-through to see if he could find any clue to the thief's identity—unfortunately, there was nothing—Bart admonished Alcina for not locking her doors. Alcina promised that would never happen again.

Seemingly in a protective mode, Reed seconded the promise.

To Bart's suggestion about installing burglar deterrents on her first-floor windows, Alcina just listened. She didn't want to feel as if she was back in New York City with its record for crime, for heaven's sake.

She had no doubts this had been a one-time happening.

Even so, Bart said he'd file his own official report with the local sheriff's department and called to get a deputy out to talk to her. The man arrived within a half hour, and while Alcina gave her statement, she noticed Pru arrive. After the deputy left, she and Josie and the brothers Quarrels helped Alcina get the place back in shape.

When the others were getting ready to leave, Reed asked, "Do you want to spend the night here? I'll sleep in any bed you designate."

"Not tonight," she said. "I'm still too spooked, I guess. I wouldn't be comfortable. Let's go back to your place."

"I didn't think you found the trailer all that comfortable."

"I don't. But at least I feel safe there."

Where, maybe by some miracle, they'd share the lumps of his only bed.

"All right," Reed agreed, "but I have some things to take care of on the spread." He glanced out the window where his brothers were getting into Chance's pickup. "Gotta go." He started backing off from her. "I won't be back at the trailer until dark."

Alcina followed him. "I'll run a few errands then and meet you there later. What time would you like dinner?"

"Around seven...seven-thirty. You're really gonna cook for me?"

"I *am* your wife, remember."

He arched his eyebrows. "Hmm, I guess your cooking supper is a start."

Then he gave her a quick kiss on the cheek and

raced out the door just in time to jump in the back of the pickup that was already pulling away.

And Alcina realized that Pru was still there.

"So how did it go last night?"

"Didn't."

"Uh...what happened?"

Despite her embarrassment, Alcina explained. It would be a sad day if she couldn't confide in her best friend.

"You can't let this go on too long," Pru said.

"I want to feel like it's more than business with Reed when we make love. I want him to care for me."

"The blind leading the blind."

"What?"

"Reed may not be madly in love with you...yet...but I saw how he was looking at you. He was worried. He cares. He's teetering and it's up to you to topple him."

"He's not a tree, for heaven's sake. He's a man."

"Right. You have that going for you. He's only a man."

IF THE WAY to a man's heart was really through his stomach, Alcina was ready to topple Reed with succulent roast loin of pork, mouthwatering oven-crisped potato chunks, garden-fresh green beans with a butter-lemon sauce and almond slivers, and the pièce de résistance, homemade apple pie. Which admittedly she'd baked at her own home. The trailer oven was hardly big enough to hold the main meal.

As if that wasn't enough ammunition, she'd dressed up the trailer, making it more homey, more romantic. Candles glowed from every niche possible, including from the table that she'd covered with a pretty patterned cloth and a basket of fresh flowers.

And she'd dressed in a simple, low-cut, long-sleeved taupe knit dress that flowed from the hip to her calves. The material clung so closely to every curve that normal underwear was out of the question. Seamless panty hose would have to do, but the trailer was so tight that she feared she'd catch the nylon on something. Better to wait until she was finished getting everything ready, then put them on.

For once, Alcina had let her hair down. She'd brushed and brushed it until it shimmered in waves around her face and shoulders.

Now, if only she could do that figuratively with Reed—let her hair down, that was. He seemed to push her ''bristle'' buttons without even trying. She needed to learn to relax around him, make soft jokes rather than stiff censure when he managed to put up her back.

Throughout her efforts to ready herself and the trailer, she'd had constant company, a companion she could talk to without having to edit herself. Temporary had dogged her every movement like a shadow, and she'd found herself responding to the mutt. Already attached to Temporary, Alcina hoped that Reed had accepted permanent responsibility.

Adjusting the position of the flowers and candles on the tiny table for the umpteenth time, Alcina asked the dog, ''What do you think, Temporary? Do you approve?''

Temporary's tail thumped the floor.

But it was a man's voice that said, ''I approve.''

An immediate warmth shot through Alcina despite the chill wind that swept into the space with Reed's arrival. She turned to find him standing in the doorway, hat in hand, his expression bemused as he looked around at what had until now been a man's domain.

The dog bounded toward him as he said, "Honey, I'm home."

"Good. Now close the door, please!"

The chill had swept her, and being half-naked with nothing at all separating the knit from her body, her flesh had responded quite naturally. Her nipples were tight buds, and she feared that Reed would notice.

She couldn't tell whether he did or not as he pulled the door closed behind him.

Temporary was practically turning herself inside out for Reed's attention. Sort of like she was, Alcina admitted, watching Reed hang his Stetson and jacket on a peg next to the door, then hunker down to give Temporary the affection the dog so obviously craved.

Alcina could use some of that herself.

And when Reed straightened and walked over to her, Alcina imagined she might just get it.

Her pulse skittered as Reed reached out...then thunked in disappointment when he kept right on reaching past her to snatch a roll from the basket.

"I'm starving," he declared, biting into the roll. "Mmm, delicious."

"Then go wash up. Dinner's ready."

"Smells good." Then, before moving on, he murmured, "And so do you."

A thrill shot through her and she watched him walk away from her. Waited until he'd disappeared into the impossibly small bathroom. Then she set the butter and a dish with the beans on the table. After which she removed the platter holding the roast and potatoes from the oven where she'd been keeping them warm.

Closing the oven door with her hip, Alcina found she couldn't move forward. Some of the material of her dress had caught between oven and door.

"Oh, no!" There simply wasn't enough space to set down the platter.

"Problem?" Reed asked as he came out of the bathroom.

"I'm stuck."

"So, I'll unstick you." He moved behind her, saying, "If you dressed appropriately, this wouldn't have happened."

Wondering how he thought underwear would make a difference—realizing she'd never gotten around to pulling on those panty hose—she said, "I always dress appropriately."

"For your place, yes. For the trailer, jeans and a T-shirt would do."

"I don't even own a pair of jeans."

"Then you ought to think about getting some." Directly behind her, he was practically breathing in her ear. As he cracked the oven door, he purposely ran a hand down her hip and thigh before freeing the material. "You'd look hot in a nice pair of tight, soft jeans. Especially here," he murmured, touching her derriere.

Alcina *was* hot. Correction, make that flaming!

Reed's intimate touch had scrambled her hormones and she feared that, if he told her to forget dinner and come to bed with him right now, she would.

Only he didn't. Trailing his hand around her waist, he circled her and slid into his side of the booth.

Obviously, his hunger for food was the more urgent

of his appetites, Alcina thought in disgust. Not that she wanted to do anything intimate with him if he was just performing his husbandly duty, of course. Nor if he was merely relieving those natural urges he'd talked about.

Irritated that Reed had set her on edge so easily—worse, while he seemed to be enjoying himself immensely—Alcina took refuge in silence as she served the meal. She felt his gaze on her every moment.

Waiting until they were eating, she finally broached what she figured to be a safe subject. "Did you ever get to finish the discussion with your father and brothers that I interrupted this morning?"

"Nope. We decided that now was not the time to make any fast decisions. We all have some thinking to do first."

He gave her the short version of what had been going on when she'd walked in.

"So all the terrible things that have been happening on the ranch haven't been bad luck at all."

"Nope. Someone is trying to drive us out and get hold of the land," he said darkly.

"Have you talked to the authorities?"

"We haven't gotten that far. I suspect, though, that Bart will want to handle it."

"So, you have any suspicions about who might be doing this to you?"

"A couple. Cesar Cardona is looking for his next acquisition. And Vernon Martell has already made Pa an offer that he refused outright."

"Odd…"

"What is?"

"Cardona and Martell," she said. "Reba's funeral.

Did you notice Cardona didn't show, and after escorting Reba to the wedding?''

''That is odd. You would think that he would at least have paid his respects.''

''They did have a fight the day before and he went home without her, but—''

''Over what?'' Reed interrupted.

''The diamond Reba found. He was acting like she shouldn't be trying to give it away. Like *he* wanted it.''

''The very same diamond that's now missing?''

Alcina frowned. ''We don't know that. Daddy did say that he'd take it and put it in a safe-deposit box for me.''

''About Reba's funeral, what were you going to say about Martell?''

''Just that Vernon Martell was the last mourner to leave the grave site. And that he put a rose on her coffin.''

''Reba always had lots of admirers.''

''So Pru said.'' She shook her head. ''I don't even know where I was going with this. It's just that you mentioned the two of them and the funeral came to mind.''

''But there doesn't seem to be a connection.''

''No.'' Her mind on the consequences to the Curly-Q, she asked, ''All the bad things that have been happening around the spread—is the family corporation in trouble?''

''Big time.''

''Enough to break up?''

''That's a distinct possibility,'' Reed admitted. ''Not that it's what I want.''

Then what would happen between her and Reed? Alcina wondered, stunned and trying not to panic.

Reed would have to go elsewhere to find work. And they didn't have the kind of relationship that would make her comfortable giving up her bed-and-breakfast to follow him blindly. Somehow, she'd never considered that she might have to face this possibility.

Appetite gone, she picked at her food.

"Now Pa's being a real pain," Reed said, the discussion not seeming to have affected his appetite. "He's up and disappeared."

"Disappeared?"

"To worry us, I guess. Make us wonder if something happened to him."

"How do you know it hasn't?"

"He's a master at manipulation," Reed assured her. "He's made us think he's been dying all this time…" He snorted in disgust. "When no one goes looking for him, he'll come home on his own. He did drive one of the pickups out when we were cleaning up your place. But he didn't even say a word to Felice. He just took off. It won't surprise me to find him in his own bed in the morning, though."

"I hope you're right." Alcina frowned. "I haven't been able to get hold of Daddy, either. Not that I've tried since I got here, of course, which was early this afternoon. Unfortunately, I don't have a cell phone."

"Me, neither. But if you're worried, after supper we could go to the house to try tracking him down."

"Oh, I'm probably stewing over nothing. Daddy is an adult, after all. He has his own life. It's just strange that he wouldn't have gone into work right from here. It's not like him to vary his routine much. I'm sure

I'll get him in the morning, though, either at home or at the bank.''

Then maybe she could convince her father to do something to take the financial pressure off the Curly-Q. She would insist on it. If the brothers had extra time, they could work out a solution. Together.

"Whatever pleases you," Reed said.

Alcina decided that he was pleasing her by respecting her worries and her wishes. Maybe Pru was right in thinking they merely needed some up-close-and-personal time to seal their relationship.

She was even more convinced when Reed turned the conversation to the past and related stories about growing up between Bart and Chance. While amused, she also felt a little sad. Overshadowed by his brothers, Reed had never been given his due in the family.

Since they were talking about the past, Alcina broached a subject she'd been curious about for years.

"Say, whatever happened between you and Barbara Jean Vogler?"

"Nothing."

"Something must have happened," she insisted. Something pretty significant. "Last I heard before going back to New York was that you were engaged."

"That lasted all of…five weeks, I think it was. Our fathers kind of pushed us together, and it seemed like we would work out pretty well, both of us being from ranch stock and all. But when I got to know her better, I realized Barbara Jean wasn't for me."

"Why not?"

What fault could the perfect woman who could ride horses and rope cattle and who probably knew how to shoot a gun have had? Alcina wondered.

Five weeks.

She considered the irony of the leap she'd taken into Jeffrey's arms. By the time she'd married him, Barbara Jean had been history for Reed.

"Barbara Jean didn't have an honest bone in her body," he explained. "Anything she thought might bother me, she conveniently forgot to mention. Or she made up some stupid story to cover herself. She was a practiced liar. It was simply annoying at first, and I thought once I faced her with it, told her that I was wise to her, that she would stop. Only she didn't. And so I didn't marry her. I couldn't live with a woman who couldn't trust me and our relationship enough to be honest," he said.

Reminding Alcina of her own dishonesty. Her failed marriage that she'd forgotten to mention now hung over her head like the sword of Damocles, ready to drop at a moment's notice.

And the feeling stayed with her when, dinner finished, Reed helped her clear the table and the already small space shrank in size. They couldn't move without brushing or bumping against each other.

While Alcina wasn't immune to the physical contact, she found herself riddled with guilt and unable to take advantage of the situation.

Having done as many of the dishes as the limited sink area allowed, Alcina turned and Reed was there, hovering mere inches from her.

Suddenly, her breath was gone and she backed up against the cabinets as if the extra inches would fix things for her. Maybe it would have if Reed didn't home right in on her.

"I want to thank you for a wonderful supper, Mrs. Quarrels." He placed his hands on the sink, one on either side of her. "You went beyond the call of duty. Why?"

He'd physically trapped her. With his presence. With his heat. She couldn't move a millimeter without rubbing up against him.

"It was just a meal," she said, trying not to sound as if she was choking over the words.

He shook his head. "I don't believe that."

She thought quickly. "Okay, so I wanted to thank you for being so caring this morning." That was at least part of the truth. "I wanted you to know I appreciated the way you took over and made me feel better."

"I'm your husband now."

"Yes," she said, breathless again. "You are."

"And that's it?"

"Isn't that enough?" she asked sharply.

He grinned. "I'll let you off the hook."

"Don't do me any favors."

"All right. I won't. I'll let you show me your appreciation with more than food."

"What then?"

"How about a little bit of you?"

Alcina should have been ready for the kiss, but she wasn't really. She'd set it up from the moment she'd walked into the trailer—the atmosphere, the food, her—and yet she wasn't prepared in some basic way.

Perhaps the lack of underwear…

With Reed kissing her, the heat of his body burning her, she felt utterly exposed. Naked. And there wasn't a thing she could do about it.

If she even wanted to…

She didn't budge when he explored her mouth with his tongue, and her hips with his hands. Pressed into her, his physical response was obvious and she couldn't prevent the responding curl deep in her stomach or the way she shifted her pelvis toward him for maximum contact.

He rocked what seemed to be his substantial length against her, slid one hand up her side to her breast and to the material that stretched and slid easily over her shoulder. He freed a breast and she moaned into his mouth as he manipulated the tight bud of her nipple.

"No bra," he murmured into her mouth. "I was right. Couldn't think about much else all through dinner."

So he had noticed, after all.

His other hand was reaching down, tugging up her skirt hem an inch at a time. Soon, he was exploring the length of her thigh...the curve of her hip...the indentation of her belly.

Then he dipped lower, his clever fingers finding and seducing her halfway to mindless.

Part of her protested that this wasn't what she wanted, not yet. Not without some admission on his part that their marriage meant more than business to him. But the other part silently urged him to take her right there on the sink among the dishes.

Suddenly, he stopped touching her, but before she could protest, both of his hands were around her waist, lifting her. His mouth found her exposed breast and he pressed his body between her thighs to make her open to him.

She clasped his back...circled his neck with her hands...ran her fingers down his spine.

Then he broke contact again and moved his head lower to taste the wet warmth between her thighs.

The motion of his tongue pinned Alcina mentally, while physically her buttocks raised from the sink on their own. A natural response to the immense pleasure he offered. Moaning, Alcina pressed herself into Reed's mouth, rocking and wrapping her legs around his back, silently urging him to explore her more fully.

He accommodated her if only with tongue and fingers. But the result was an explosion of the highest magnitude. Waves of pleasure washed through her as she tumbled down from the heights and into his waiting grasp.

Before she knew what he was up to, he lifted her in his arms and fought with the narrow doorway so that he could carry her into the bedroom. He kissed her long and lingering, then set her on the bed.

Weak-limbed, Alcina was nevertheless ready for anything. She sprawled back and opened her arms to receive Reed's weight when he joined her.

Joined with her...

"Sweet dreams," he whispered, backing off instead.

"That's it?"

He hesitated in the doorway. "Are you inviting me to sleep in the bed with you?"

She wanted him to. But she also wanted to hear the magic words.

Not that the words had to be *I love you.*

He could choose so many ways to express his affection and regard that would reassure her.

But he said nothing.

So neither did she.

Reed waited barely a moment before backing out of the room and drawing the privacy curtain.

And Alcina covered her face with a pillow so he wouldn't hear her frustrated wail.

EVEN BEFORE he got into his vehicle, he knew he was being watched.

No one could dupe him so easily. Not when he was forever on guard.

Forever watching. Waiting. Biding his time.

No sooner had he pulled out of the parking spot than he saw the headlights of the other vehicle turn on. To make certain that he didn't lose his tail, he drove slower than he normally would.

Reveling in games of chance ran in his blood. And wasn't his the ultimate game? He'd been playing for quite a while, and only now was someone catching on.

That damn diamond had given him away just as he knew it would!

The headlights in his rearview mirror receded. Trying to hoodwink him into thinking he wasn't being followed, after all? He wasn't so naive.

He had a plan, he was good at thinking on his feet. Not the most clever of plans, perhaps, but it would do.

It wasn't long before he turned onto an utterly dark, deserted gravel road. He traveled along this for nearly a mile before turning onto one more primitive, littered with debris and potholes.

He knew the vehicle behind him followed, even as he knew exactly when the headlights were cut. Knew that it was done to fool him.

But he was no fool.

He knew he wasn't alone.

Once he'd parked the car, he took his time getting

out and retrieving the flashlight and rifle from the back. The weapon was already loaded. And he was expert at its use. Listening hard, he caught the purr of an engine nearby before it, too, abruptly died.

The silence made him smile. As did the creak of a metal hinge.

He moved forward, shining his light broadly so that the trail he took couldn't be missed.

The place had been closed up for years before he'd come to claim it. It had been and still was unsafe inside. Exactly how he liked it. Dangerous footing. Rotted wood. A ceiling that threatened to cave in at the first sharp sound.

But he had made the place his own. With unlimited time to explore every nook and cranny, he knew where to hide, just as he knew where the most danger lay.

Deep inside his lair, he grinned, confident that he wouldn't be alone for long.

The wait didn't bother him.

His prey would never see daylight again.

Chapter Ten

Reed went from aggravated to concerned when he and Alcina got to the house the next morning only to discover that Pa was still gone.

"Not even a telephone call?" Reed asked Felice.

"Not a word, Mr. Reed."

"Telephone," Alcina echoed. "I'm going to check on Daddy. I'll use the phone in the office."

She rushed out of the kitchen where Reed poured himself a mug of coffee, strong and black.

"I am worried," Felice said. "Mr. Emmett is a stubborn man...but where could he have been all this time?"

"I don't have a clue."

"And Mr. Bart already took Daniel and Lainey to Albuquerque. He was very angry with your father." She hesitated a moment before informing him, "And he means to meet with Sheriff Olvera this morning."

Reed's gut tightened. Did that mean that Bart planned to sell out and go back to his old job?

"He'll do what he has to," Reed said tightly. "And I'll do what I have to. I can handle Pa."

"If you can find him." As she straightened up an already clean kitchen, Felice muttered to herself in

Spanish. Then she made a sound of exasperation and asked, "Can I fix you breakfast, Mr. Reed?"

"Thanks, but I don't seem to have an appetite this morning."

Besides, his stomach was churned up from his stewing.

What was Pa up to now?

The old man had everyone worried about him, which had become his specialty lately. Maybe he was sitting back, enjoying himself, thinking they were all running around in circles, like chickens with their heads cut off, trying to find him.

Reed vowed that he'd figure it out, but he wasn't going to drop everything to do so. With Bart already gone and Chance planning to leave for the rodeo by early afternoon, the welfare of the ranch was solely in his hands and would be for at least a few days. He wasn't about to neglect the place.

Who knew how much longer he would be able to call it his?

And after all, Pa had left of his own volition. There had been no indication of foul play, so why should he think the worst? No doubt this was Pa's ploy to deflect his guilt in fooling them all.

Well, the old man had cried wolf once too often…

Reed went in search of Alcina, who was just hanging up the telephone with what looked like nerveless fingers. She appeared pale and tense.

"No luck?"

She shook her head. "Daddy hasn't even called the bank or collected his messages from his answering machine. And he hasn't left a message for me, either. This isn't like him, Reed. What the heck is going on?"

"Both of our fathers missing…a coincidence? I wonder."

"What?"

"They were having a set-to yesterday, but after I broke it up, they insisted that I leave them be because they had some things to discuss."

"And when I barged in on your family meeting," Alcina said, "I heard your father talking to himself, something about a partner selling out. At the time, I didn't know what he was talking about…then I figured he meant one of you."

"But maybe he meant Tucker."

"So you think they could be together? But where? And to what purpose?"

"I don't know. And I'm gonna be real ticked if I leave the work on the ranch and find they've been playing some damn game with us. Rather, if Pa has."

"What about the authorities?"

"Sheriff's department won't do anything this soon—it hasn't even been twenty-four hours. They're adults with their full faculties—at least your daddy has his—and there's no indication of foul play."

"Oh, right."

Alcina appeared so forlorn, Reed wanted to take her in his arms and comfort her, but he knew what that could lead to. He didn't think he would be able to sacrifice his growing need for her once aroused again.

Sighing, Reed caved from his determined position not to be drawn into Pa's new game.

"All right, all right. I'll tell you what I'll do. I can make a few calls to the neighboring ranches, see if anyone has set eyes on either of them. Put the word out that if anyone does, to let us know immediately.

But that's not going to reach everyone, not by a long shot.''

It was the best concession he could make at the moment. And it seemed to please Alcina, who suddenly seemed as if a burden had been lifted from her shoulders. As if he would let her go through this alone, even if his own pa weren't involved.

"We could ask around ourselves in town," Alcina said excitedly.

"Later, maybe." He had to draw a line somewhere. "And we still don't know that they're together. What if your father's car simply broke down on the way home? Do you know his emergency service?"

Alcina brightened. "I know the route he takes. I think I'll go for a drive. If I find him, I'll call. If I don't, I'll be back in a couple of hours."

"You're planning on going alone?"

She blinked and her eyes widened. "You have a problem with that?"

"Hey, I'm not telling you what to do. I would just feel better if you wouldn't go alone."

What kind of trouble she could get herself into, Reed couldn't say. And he didn't want to consider too closely why he should worry so much about her in the first place.

"I am a big girl."

"A fact that you drove home last night."

"*I* did? You were in the driver's seat!"

"As I recall, you were the one who wore a dress with no underwear," he said, discomfort immediately growing at the vivid memory.

Her mouth snapped shut and color flooded her face. Reed had never seen her look more desirable. He wanted nothing more than to take her into his arms for an up-close-and-personal reminder.

But danger lay in that path. He didn't need another distraction.

"I'll make the calls, after which I have work to get to," he said. "If you learn anything of interest, let me know and I'll come running."

ALCINA WAS MUSING over Reed's seemingly protective nature when she arrived at the Garner place. Chance was in the yard, keeping an eye on Hope, who was playing with Pru's nieces.

Waving to him, Alcina let herself in. Pru was in the midst of packing.

"Well, how did it go?"

"Swimmingly. Reed was ready to have sex with me and didn't even mention the words *business* or *duty.*"

"That's progress. So did you?"

"Not exactly…" Before Pru could demand details, Alcina said, "I need a favor."

"Ask."

"Can I borrow a pair of jeans?"

"Jeans? For…?"

"For me, of course. I thought I'd try some, see if I like them before I bought a pair."

Pru's eyebrows shot right up practically to her hairline. "Okeydoke. How tight do you want them?"

"How tight do you have?"

Alcina had never before lain prostrate on a bed to zip up a pair of pants. There was a first time for everything, she decided.

Unable to breathe, she nevertheless rose and inspected herself from all angles in a mirror. Hmm, she could see why Reed wanted her to wear them.

"They'll do," she croaked, thinking they looked good with her buttoned cashmere sweater tucked inside.

"Practice talking or Reed'll be more hung up on the fact that you have some weird vocal problem than he will be on your butt. Don't worry, they'll loosen up a little with wear."

Alcina changed back into her skirt and a camel-hair jacket. The jeans could wait until later. Much later. She could only go without breathing properly for so long.

Hugging Pru, Alcina left, trophy jeans in hand. Chance was still outside with the girls.

"Good luck in the competitions!" she called.

"Thanks. Has anyone heard from Pa?"

"Not yet. But we'll find him," she said confidently, certain that Reed could do anything he put his mind to.

Alcina then took off and went in search of her father. She drove slower than usual so as not to miss Tucker's car if he'd turned off the road. But she saw not a single breakdown all the way into Taos.

When she arrived at her father's house, she used her own set of keys to let herself in. The place was empty, the mailbox full. He hadn't been there.

Alcina checked his answering machine—all four messages had been from her. She called herself. No messages at all. She called the bank. No one there had heard from him.

Then, as a last resort, she went into her father's study and searched his files until she found his personal records. In no time, she had the name and number of his emergency road service. But, immediately checking, she learned that he hadn't called them for help.

Alcina told herself not to panic. She assured herself that nothing terrible had happened to her father.

Undoubtedly, his disappearance, concurrent with Emmett's, hadn't been coincidence. The former partners must be together. They would watch each others' backs. At least she hoped they would.

And she and Reed would find them.

Exhausted, not having slept well the night before with Reed in the next room close enough to touch, Alcina lay down on the couch and closed her eyes for just a minute…

…a vision of Reed as she'd seen him the night before while in the throes of passion whirled through her head…

By the time she opened her eyes again, the sun was setting. She'd slept for hours.

Half-panicked, she called Reed.

"Have you heard anything?" she asked the moment Felice got him on the phone.

"Nothing. Sorry. You?"

"No. Daddy didn't have his car towed by his emergency service, either. I checked. Now what?"

"Now we ask everyone we can. Let's meet at the Silver Slipper around seven."

"You want to meet in a bar?"

"Unfortunately, Reba's Café is closed for the immediate present," he reminded her. "Unless the gas station is more to your liking. But I'm not sure how many old cowboys we could question actually hang around the pumps."

"The Silver Slipper it is," she agreed.

Before leaving her father's home, she showered and changed, once more prostrating herself to zip up the jeans. Hopefully, the effort would be worth the discomfort—she felt as if she'd been poured into them.

On her way to Silver Springs, she noticed her gas tank was nearly empty. According to the clock, she had plenty of time. The gas station would be her first stop, after all.

Getting out of the car was a relief. She could breathe normally again as she filled her tank and went inside to pay. It was on her way out, when she chose to use the bathroom around back, that she spotted the old pickup parked directly behind the building.

It was dark and hard to see, but she stopped and stared at the rusting vehicle, anyway, wondering what it was doing back here.

The gas station had a small parking area to one side out front. A truck had been parked there. Certainly, that one belonged to Hal Jenks, the cashier, for she'd seen no one else around.

The abandoned vehicle kept her wondering while she used the bathroom and fought with the jeans once more.

When she stepped back outside, Alcina couldn't help herself. Circling the pickup, she looked for something that would indicate the owner. The license plates weren't personalized and therefore of no help.

Only one option left to her...

People rarely locked their vehicles in these parts, and whoever had driven the pickup was no exception. Pulse threading unevenly at her own daring, she opened the passenger door and slid into the dusty interior, then went straight for the glove compartment.

Digging around, she found a flashlight, and then the vehicle registration. Flushing with excitement, she confirmed the pickup belonged to the Curly-Q, one of many, she knew.

Undoubtedly, this particular vehicle was the very one that Emmett Quarrels had driven off the spread the day before!

But why had he left it here at the edge of town? And where the heck had he gone? And was her father with him?

She flashed the light along the ground next to the pickup. Sure enough, tire tracks. The ground had been wet from the snow the day before, so it was a safe bet the men had met here.

Hoping for some answers from the cashier, she ran back inside the gas station.

"Hey, Hal, the pickup that's parked behind the building, did Emmett Quarrels leave it here?"

"What pickup?"

The cashier's expression was blank as if he didn't know what she was talking about. Did that mean the vehicle had been left there since the man had come on shift?

"Have you been around back today?" she asked.

"Nope."

"What about yesterday?"

"No reason to."

"You don't use the bathroom back there?"

He pointed to a nearby door. "We have an Employees Only."

So it probably wouldn't do any good to question anyone else who'd worked the past two days, either.

Frustrated, anxious to share the news with Reed, Alcina headed for the Silver Slipper, arriving a few minutes before seven. She didn't see Reed's pickup parked along the street. Preferring someplace more comfortable than her car, she went inside to wait for him.

Hugh Ruskin spotted her immediately and sauntered away from a customer toward her. He leaned his elbows on the bar and grinned, the expression making her stomach tighten. His pale eyes pinned her.

"Well, I'll be, if it isn't the new Mrs. Quarrels," he said in a too-personal tone almost too low to hear over the cacophony of voices and blaring music. "Lost your husband already?"

"I'm meeting him here."

Ruskin was putting her on the immediate defensive, Alcina realized. Uncomfortable, she looked around for an empty table, but with Reba's Café closed, the Silver Slipper was the only game in town.

The place was packed, mostly with men.

There was no helping it—Alcina slid onto the bar stool nearest the door.

"What can I get you?"

"Make it a margarita. Lots of salt and lime, easy on the tequila."

Pulling off her jacket, she swiveled her stool to get a better look at the room's occupants and was a little surprised to see Cesar Cardona and Vernon Martell at the same table, heads together, deep in what looked to be a heated discussion.

While Cardona was dressed in another gaucho-type suit plainer than the one he'd worn to the wedding, Martell wore his work clothes—jeans, flannel shirt and lined vest.

She wondered what the two dissimilar men had in common other than their romantic trysts with Reba

Gantry before she died. Then Alcina remembered they'd had business dealings before. Cardona had bought out Luis Gonzalez to develop Land of Enchantment Acres, but he'd first resold half of the acreage to Martell.

She couldn't help wondering if they had another deal in the works—one that concerned the Curly-Q Ranch.

"Here you go."

She turned back to the bar as Ruskin slid her margarita glass toward her, his hand heavy with gold rings.

"See if that's to your liking."

Alcina took a sip. "Perfect."

Her gaze wandered back to his rings and she realized she was automatically looking for an empty setting in the shape of a triangle.

"See anything you like?"

Startled, she shot her gaze to his. "What?"

"The rings." He held out both hands. He was wearing seven in total. "I collect them. This one's my favorite."

Oddly enough, he pointed to the least expensive of the bunch on the middle finger of his left hand. The only silver ring, it looked like a river of twisted metal.

"It is interesting."

"The silver came from ore right out of the old Silver Springs mine, or so I was told. You never know who to trust."

Caught by his strange intonation and direct expression, she just stared.

"Are you sure that margarita's all right?" he asked. "I can make a new one if you don't like it."

"No, it's great." She took a long, fortifying swallow, then asked, "Is that what brought you to Silver Springs?"

"What? A ring? Hardly. Silver Springs seemed like a quiet town and I was looking for quiet."

She'd meant the mine itself, but his answer made her wonder if he equated quiet with a place to hide out. From Josie's account, Hugh Ruskin was a tough customer who'd gotten the best of Bart.

Thinking she should get back to the business that brought her here, she casually asked, "Say, Emmett Quarrels hasn't stopped by lately, has he?"

"Old Emmett? Nah. He's never been in here since I took over the place. I understand he's got a bad heart. Can't drink." As if he'd been paged, Ruskin glanced down to the other end of the bar. "Hang on, gotta take care of another customer."

Relieved that she was no longer the center of his close scrutiny, Alcina decided to invite herself to sit with Cesar Cardona and Vernon Martell. Maybe she could get some hint of what they were plotting.

As she moved closer, however, they dropped any talk of business and, as if one, looked up at her questioningly.

"I was wondering if you gentlemen would mind my joining you until Reed gets here?" Alcina asked the men, giving them her sweetest smile.

"Not at all, Alcina." Ever the gentleman, Cardona rose and pulled out a chair for her. "Pardon me, that's Señora Quarrels, now, yes?"

"Alcina will do."

She sat and smiled at Martell, who removed his hat and set it on the table, but said nothing to her directly. She set her jacket on the remaining unoccupied chair.

"Bartender!" Cardona waved a hand in Ruskin's direction. "We need a fresh round at this table."

Ruskin moved around the bar, asking, "What can I get you?" but he was staring at her in a way that made her skin crawl.

"I don't need another drink," Alcina told him.

"But I insist," Cardona said. "Then we can make a toast to the bride."

"All right, you talked me into it." Figuring that complying would get Cardona in more of an expansive mood than refusing, she said, "Another margarita, then."

She didn't have to finish the first. Or the second for that matter. She was already feeling pleasantly mellow. But a sip to appease the man wouldn't hurt.

"And you gentlemen?"

"Margaritas all around," Cardona said. "And put it on my bill."

Alcina waited until Ruskin had gone back to the bar to pour their drinks before asking, "So what brings you here tonight?"

"Now that Reba's Café has closed its doors, the Silver Slipper is the pulse of the community," Cardona said. "And I plan to be part of this community for a very long time."

Alcina stared at him. Not a word about Reba herself. She could hardly believe that he was so callous.

Clearing her throat, she turned to Martell. "What about you?"

"My wife. Staring at the television night after night with her gets to me," the rancher said defiantly. "The wife's an invalid, you know. She can't do much else other than eat and sleep." Before Alcina could offer some expression of sympathy, he turned the tables on her. "And what brings you here?"

"My husband. He and I are on a fact-finding mission. Make that a father-finding mission," she said, keeping her tone light. "When was the last time either of you gentlemen saw Emmett Quarrels?"

"What? He's missing?" Martell asked, sounding truly surprised.

"He, uh, had a disagreement with his sons yesterday and did a little disappearing act, no doubt to worry them."

"Sounds like Quarrels," Martell said.

"So, have either of you seen him?"

"Not since the wedding last week," Cardona offered.

And when she looked to Martell, he said, "Reba's funeral."

The ensuing silence was deafening.

Like Hugh Ruskin, they were both fairly new to the community. Neither was likely to know her father, so she didn't mention him.

Instead, she asked, "What time do you have?" She was becoming impatient to see Reed.

Cardona checked his watch, a simple piece with plain leather band. She wondered that he didn't wear the jeweled one that he'd so proudly shown off at the wedding.

"Ten past seven," he announced.

"Hmm. Reed is late."

And she desperately needed an excuse to get away from the table for a minute. The tension was getting to her.

"Listen, I'll be right back," she said, popping out

of her chair. "I need to call Reed to see what's holding him up."

The pay phone was out of sight of the bar, down a hallway that also led to the bathrooms and a rear exit. Alcina made her way to the phone carefully—the effect of the margarita had already sneaked up on her.

Having shoved a slender wallet into one of her pockets, she was pleased to find that it slipped out without difficulty. The jeans were loosening. She dug out the coins and dropped them into the slot, then dialed.

Felice answered. "Curly-Q."

"This is Alcina. Is Reed still there?"

"He was running late, Miss Alcina. He returned to the trailer to shower and change. But he should be in town soon."

"Thanks, Felice."

Hanging up, she returned the wallet back into her pocket. Her fingers fumbled slightly, but she managed it.

When she got back to the table, the drinks had already been delivered. And Cardona was sitting alone.

"Where's your friend?" she asked, knowing Martell wasn't in the bathroom because he hadn't passed her.

"He downed half his drink and said he had to leave." Cardona shrugged and lifted his glass. "To the beautiful bride," he toasted.

Prompting her to pick up the fresh margarita. The first glass was nowhere to be seen. The salty-tart taste was even more appealing than before. Thirsty, she downed a long swallow.

"What brought you to Silver Springs?" she asked Cardona.

"My business, of course."

"I mean in the first place. Why did you choose to build here? Did you ever live in this area?"

"A long time ago, yes," he admitted. "But only for a few years when I was a small child. My reasons to build here were strictly business, though. The price of the land was right. And Silver Springs is close enough to Taos and Angelfire to be attractive to people who want to pursue both culture and winter sports."

"You really thought it through."

"That's the way I approach everything, Alcina. With my head. And with great patience. That's the key to success. I've waited a long, long time to get what I deserve out of life."

Alcina lost focus on what he was saying and suddenly realized that she must have consumed too much alcohol. Not that she'd even finished the drink in front of her. But her eyes were getting heavy and her brain a little fuzzy.

"To getting things we deserve," Cardona said, lifting his drink to toast with her.

Alcina put her hand around her glass, then changed her mind. "Whoa. I think I'd better stop right there."

"And force me to drink alone?"

"If I don't switch to tonic water, Reed'll have to carry me out of here."

"Your pleasure is mine," Cardona said. "Bartender, a tonic water for the lady."

"Coming right up."

Alcina's limbs were growing heavier by the second, and she wanted nothing more than to close her eyes.

"Um, I think I'll go splash some water on my face."

She had to place her hands on the table to push herself up. Unsteady, she stood there for a moment, willing the room to stop spinning...and her stomach to stop churning. She was feeling sick as well as drunk.

"I—I'll be back," she muttered.

Somehow, Alcina made it to the hallway. Then she was able to feel her way along the walls. The distance seemed enormous to her. She thought she'd never make it.

Each step took her down...down...down farther into a truly wretched state.

What had happened to make her feel so terrible? Alcina wondered as she stumbled into the bathroom.

She made it to the sink and managed to turn on the cold-water faucet. Margaritas had never done this to her before. One might make her silly. Two—her limit—might get her a little drunk, but certainly not sick.

And, boy was she sick! And she hadn't even finished either of her drinks.

All the cold water in the world on her wrists and face didn't help to bring her around.

The effects kept increasing but she couldn't keep fighting them.

Alcina felt herself fading...barely able to remain on her feet, grasping the sink with both hands for all she was worth. Too weak.

No more margaritas for her!

Her last thought as her fingers gave and she ungraciously sank to the bathroom floor...

...rough hands under her arms brought her halfway back to consciousness, if unable to force her eyes open...

She was being dragged.

Jostled.

Thrown.

Pain flared in waves through her already sore hip and shoulder.

She struggled upward, when the rough hands returned, this time touching her body all over.

She fought the invasion...tried to open her eyes...barely caught a glimpse of a large man's silhouette looming over her.

Sharp pain in her jaw made her see stars...

Then nothing at all.

REED PARKED his truck down the block from the Silver Slipper and strode quickly toward the place. Nearly half an hour late—Alcina would be fit to be tied.

If she'd even waited for him. She was an expert at being prickly.

Spotting her car parked nearby reassured him. But when he walked into the bar, he didn't see his wife.

Catching Ruskin's attention, he asked, "Has Alcina been in?"

"For the past hour or so." Ruskin turned his gaze to the tables. "Hmm. Last I saw her, she was sitting with Cardona, over there."

"Thanks," Reed muttered. He should have known she'd start asking after his father without him.

Cesar Cardona was just rising, looking as if he was

ready to leave. Alcina's camel-hair jacket was draped over one of the other chairs.

"Ah, Reed, there you are," Cardona said with a grin. "Your wife was becoming impatient over you."

"She left without me? And without her jacket?"

"No, no. She wasn't feeling well. A little too much tequila. She went to the ladies' room a while ago."

Reed was already hotfooting it down the hall.

Arriving at the bathroom, he knocked. "Alcina? You okay?"

No answer.

He knocked again, louder, this time opening the door when there was no response.

The room was empty.

"What the hell?"

Reed backed out and stood there for a moment until he noticed the cold draft. He saw the rear door cracked open even as he heard a muffled sound from beyond.

"Alcina!"

He threw the door open, the light from the hallway faintly illuminating his wife prone in the gangway, a hulking figure over her.

"Hey!"

Like a madman, he flung himself through the doorway, aimed at the man who dared touch his wife so intimately.

They connected and went rolling, even as the other man muttered, "What the hell!"

Reed's fist connected with the man's mouth, closing it for him. They traded punches, and it was only by sheer luck that Reed got the upper hand on the bigger man, dragging him back into the light for a look.

"Martell? Explain yourself," Reed demanded as a moan broke from Alcina.

He let go of the man and flew to her side.

"I heard noises and I found her lying there," Martell boomed. "I was just trying to bring her to."

"What's going on?" came another male voice belonging to Hugh Ruskin.

But Reed was focused on his wife. "Alcina, are you all right?"

She made another sound low in her throat and turned her head toward the light. He could see that the side of her mouth was swollen, as if someone had hit her. Her eyelids fluttered and she moaned again.

"I'm here now," he said, finally noticing the disarray of her clothing. Her cashmere sweater was unbuttoned all the way to her waist and her jeans were unsnapped and unzipped. "It's Reed. I'm here. I'll take care of you. Does anything hurt?"

Reed quickly began buttoning her sweater.

She licked her lips. "Hip." She barely got the word out. And then, "Shoulder."

"What in the heck happened out here?" Ruskin asked.

"I was coming back to the bar from my truck and I heard this noise," Martell claimed. "I just found her and was trying to help her up when that madman charged me. I couldn't even see who it was, for God's sake!"

"I guess a woman who can't hold her liquor shouldn't drink," Ruskin mused.

Making Reed want to kill the bartender with his bare hands. Him and whoever attacked his wife. Alcina hadn't ended up sprawled in an alley half-undressed on her own.

He zipped her up and snapped her, and only then did he realize she was wearing jeans after claiming she didn't own a pair.

"I'm going to help you to your feet," he said, trying to sound reasonable when that was the last thing he felt like being. He wanted to punch something—*someone*—bad. "Do you think you can stand?"

"Mmm."

He had her in a sitting position before she seemed to focus on him. "Reed?"

"Yeah, I'm here. What is it? Does something hurt? Should I get you to a hospital?"

"You're late!"

With that announcement, she passed out again and began to snore.

Chapter Eleven

Bright light sizzled the backs of her eyelids, making Alcina reluctant to open them lest they hurt worse.

She hurt…all over.

What had happened to her?

She remembered being sick…roughed up…taken care of.

Her eyes flew open and she squinted for a moment until they adjusted and she could scope things out. She was in her own room, in her own bed.

Reed was there, sprawled in her rocking chair, his stocking feet on a cushioned footstool. His eyes were closed, his mouth opened slightly. She could hear his steady breathing against the quiet of the room.

Vague remembrances of the night before hit her in waves. The only thing she could be sure of was that she'd been damn sick. And that Reed had brought her home. Had taken care of her. Had watched over her all night long, from the looks of it.

She also remembered him calling Bart and his friend John Malone—the sheriff of Taos County. She thought someone had come in the middle of the night, but Reed had taken care of the situation as he had the break-in.

Carefully, she sat up. Her head throbbed and her jaw was sore, just as if someone had hit her.

Not wanting to waken Reed, she awkwardly slid to the other side of the bed away from him, every muscle of her body protesting, especially her shoulder and hip. About to get out from under the covers, she realized that she was next to naked, dressed only in her bra and panties. And she didn't remember undressing herself.

Flustered, she glanced back at Reed. His head had rolled to one side, and he continued to breathe deeply. He was still sound asleep.

Alcina left the bed and crept to the bathroom, where she inspected herself in the mirror. The left side of her lower lip was a little swollen, and a smudge of a bruise shadowed her jaw.

Someone *had* hit her!

A zipped plastic bag filled with water had been discarded in the sink. Melted ice? Vaguely, she remembered Reed holding something cold to her face…

The rest of her looked normal enough, except for the hip she'd bruised at the fire. That was now blooming anew.

She popped a couple of aspirin for the headache and turned on the shower.

Bits and pieces of memory returned as the hot water beat down on her, loosening tight, sore muscles. Someone dragging her. Being dumped. Rough hands on her body.

She just couldn't put it all together.

Only one image kept coming back to her—Reed, taking care of her.

Was it possible that he was beginning to feel something for her other than friendship?

Alcina shook her head. Knowing Reed, he would have done the same thing for any human being. Heck, he'd done as much for Temporary.

She forbade herself any maudlin thoughts. She needed to concentrate.

But no matter how hard she tried, Alcina couldn't envision exactly what had happened between her passing out in the bathroom and Reed's finding her in the street.

She stepped out of the shower, feeling both better physically and deeply shaken mentally. After drying off, she wrapped a bath sheet around herself, then ventured back into the bedroom.

Reed was awake. The sound of the shower must have penetrated his deep sleep. Standing before the window, his back was to her. But he must have sensed her presence.

"Good morning," he said and turned to face her. His gaze drifted to the towel where it bound her breasts. "You're looking better."

"I'm feeling better...I guess." Quickly, she fetched a robe from the closet and slipped it on over the towel. "Last night's kind of a blur."

"How many margaritas did you drink?"

"I wasn't drunk!" Even as she denied it, Alcina knew it to be true. "I mean, I certainly did feel a little mellow. But then I got sick and tequila doesn't make me sick. It was the weirdest feeling...like...like..."

"What?"

Finally, she put her finger on what had been troubling her. "I've had some bad reactions to medications. Anti-inflammatories, muscle relaxants. They've upset my stomach and made me feel horrible all over. That's kind of how I felt last night, only worse."

Reed's expression changed and he moved toward her. "Could someone have spiked your drink?"

"I guess it's possible…ooh, alcohol combined with a drug that didn't agree with me." She shuddered.

"Tell me everything you can remember about last night from the moment you arrived at the bar."

Alcina did her best to give him every detail. She wasn't having trouble recounting the early part of the evening.

She started with finding the pickup, went on to her conversation with Ruskin about the rings, ended with her making the telephone call and coming back to find her fresh margarita on the table.

"The first drink didn't bother you?"

"I didn't feel anything weird."

"So it was the second one that made you sick. And Martell had access to it before he left the Silver Slipper."

"Martell? Why would he have spiked my drink?"

"Your clothes," Reed said, moving close enough to brush the loose hair back from her cheek. "They were open."

Disturbed by his unexpected touch, she didn't get what he was trying to tell her. "What?"

His expression pained, Reed said, "You were lying on the ground with your sweater unbuttoned and your jeans unzipped. You were molested, and if I hadn't gotten there when I did, you might have been…it might have gone further."

Alcina was already shaking her head in denial. "Sexually molested? No. That's wrong. I would know."

"Not if you were out when it happened. I pulled

Vernon Martell off you,'' Reed finally said, wrapping his arms around her.

Alcina's pulse raced and not only due to his proximity. His *words* disturbed her. She took mental inventory of her body, but her tender parts all felt fine. No matter what it had looked like, sex hadn't been involved.

More vague memories returned in snatches, again of someone handling her roughly but not intimately. Martell? She couldn't say. But Reed had believed it and he'd gone all out to protect her.

''And you took such good care of me last night,'' she murmured, finding some good in the bad.

''Of course. You're mine.''

Alcina ignored the statement of ownership and pulled away a bit so she could look directly into his eyes. ''But I wasn't molested…I was searched.'' The more she thought about it, the more certain she was. ''The person who did this was looking for something specific.'' It came to her from nowhere. ''The diamond.''

Silence stretched between them for a moment and Alcina could tell Reed was considering that seriously. Her own mind was working at high speed.

''The diamond was gone after the break-in. What if Daddy *does* have it?'' she asked. ''The intruder didn't find it here, so he thought I had it on me.''

''How would this person know you had it in the first place? Who did you tell about it?''

''Only Daddy and Pru knew. And Reba, of course…and anyone she told.'' Alcina's heart nearly stopped with the next leap. ''Oh my God…Reba…''

''You're not thinking—''

''That Reba's death was no accident,'' Alcina said,

nodding, feeling as if she'd knocked over the first domino and the whole chain was following. Everything was starting to fall into place. "And that she died from a combination of painkillers and alcohol, probably the very thing that made me so sick! Good thing I didn't drink any more than I did."

Reed cursed. "That diamond must have been valuable, but worth killing for?"

"What if it wasn't the diamond itself? How about its worth being a 'staying out of jail' card? What if the person who set the barn fire lost the diamond in the act, then later realized it could point to him?"

"Murder to cover up a lesser crime?"

"I've heard of weirder things happening."

Reed shook his head. "There must be something much bigger at stake here."

"But how do we figure out what?" Alcina asked, frustrated by the eventual roadblock. "How do we put all the pieces of the puzzle together to make some sense of it?"

"Puzzle. That's it," Reed said, kissing her. He grabbed his boots. "Get dressed. We need to get back to the ranch to figure this thing out."

He started to leave the room, then hesitated. Turning back to her, he grinned.

"And be sure to wear those jeans you found. They look mighty fine on you, Mrs. Quarrels."

THEIR FIRST STOP was at the gas station. Reed checked out the pickup for himself.

"This is the vehicle Pa drove off the ranch, all right."

"And from these tracks," Alcina said, pointing to a set imprinted in the muck nearby, "we can hope he and Daddy are together, watching each others' backs.''

"But what in the world are they up to?" Reed shook his head. "Let's get some coffee and doughnuts, then get over to the ranch."

Reed knew he couldn't leave Alcina alone again until the mystery was solved. He could have lost her. Or she could have been seriously hurt.

Relief had washed through him at her insistence that she hadn't been sexually molested.

Thank God.

The thought had eaten at his gut like a cancer all night long. He'd tended to her needs, then tucked her in bed and settled himself close at hand, just in case she needed him.

Alcina surely inspired extreme emotions in him. Why? he wondered.

The night before, he'd wanted nothing more than to use Vernon Martell as a human punching bag. As he'd lifted Alcina into his arms, he'd threatened the rancher with dire consequences if he ever came near her again.

But maybe Martell had been telling the truth when he said he'd been trying to help Alcina.

"If Martell didn't attack you, then who?" Reed asked aloud.

"Who else wants the land?"

"Cesar Cardona."

"And Cardona was intent on Reba's not showing the diamond around," Alcina murmured. "He even offhandedly claimed it was his. And he had access to Reba herself."

"And…he had access to your drink."

"So did the bartender, for that matter."

"Except you said the first drink didn't make you sick," Reed reminded her.

"Maybe I just didn't drink enough of it. Or enough time didn't pass."

"I don't know. Hugh Ruskin doesn't seem the type to want to work too hard. I can't see him having the urge to ranch."

"True. No one else has shown interest in the Curly-Q?"

"Not that I know of."

After taking a curve on the way down to the canyon floor, Reed glanced at Alcina, who sat quiet and thoughtful. She was wearing the jeans especially for him.

Her way of telling him how she felt about him?

Reed reluctantly admitted that he did have some scary feelings for Alcina…he couldn't think of her as a business partner if his life depended on it.

So why couldn't he woo her properly? He knew that was all she wanted to make theirs a real marriage.

He guessed the circumstances surrounding his proposal sat between them like a big wedge. She didn't know the extent of the ugliness of it. And he didn't know how to get around it.

One more example of his not being able to speak his mind when it counted…

The ranch had never seemed so deserted, what with Pa missing, Bart and the kids in Albuquerque and Moon-Eye and Frank already out distributing cake— high-protein food pellets—to the herd.

Only Felice moved around the house, her manner subdued. She, too, was worried about Pa. She insisted she make them a big lunch and Reed didn't argue. It would keep her busy and they would need to eat eventually. The coffee and doughnuts wouldn't hold them much longer.

Once in the office, Reed found the ranch ledger and Pa's ranch diary, in which the old man made notations to himself about what happened and when.

"We need to make a list of all the bad luck we've been having, right from the very beginning."

"You think we can find a pattern of some kind?"

"Exactly."

That they were operating on the same track pleased Reed. While Alcina paged through the ledger, noting the unusual expenditures, Reed went through Pa's diary. He started a year back and moved forward, skimming every page.

"Here," he said. "It all started with the anthrax outbreak."

"Anthrax. You don't think that was an act of nature?"

"It wouldn't be easy to get, but labs do have vials of the anthrax virus in order to make the vaccine, so it's possible that a person was responsible. And Pa noted a call from a Realtor the very next day."

"How horrible that someone would purposely spread a deadly disease."

"You know, I can't see another rancher being responsible," Reed said, "not with the disrespect shown to the animals and property. Causing an outbreak of anthrax would not only kill cows, it would make that land unusable for grazing in his lifetime and beyond. They say there have been cases of spores infecting animals a century after the original outbreak."

"Which means you've eliminated your main suspect, Vernon Martell," Alcina said.

Reed didn't know what kind of a rancher Martell was, with him being one of the newcomers to the area, but Reed did find it difficult to believe the man could have done something so vile.

"So we're back to Cesar Cardona," Alcina murmured.

"Pa figured a land developer was involved," Reed admitted. "But I'm not so sure. Other ranchers have been willing to sell right along. There's plenty of land around for as many city slickers who want acreage. So I don't think the attraction is land development."

"Unless there's something special about the particular area…" Alcina switched gears. "Here's a big expenditure. Repairs to fences." She added it to the list.

"And a bunch of feed going moldy when it shouldn't have," Reed told her.

There was no end to the small things. Nearly none to the big. Sick cows, broken windmill, downed fence, dying calves, broken posthole digger.

At the next diary entry he read, Reed suddenly sat up straighter. "Chance's electrocution—Pa thought Will Spencer had nothing to do with that because he got one of those calls from a real estate agent the next day."

"You think whoever is responsible wanted Chance dead?"

"Chance probably wasn't the intended target. There was a downed power line crossing an electric fence. That could have killed off more than a few head."

"Instead, it almost killed your brother."

"Only because he got in the way," Reed reasoned.

Alcina's eyes went wide. "Like Peter Dagget, the

kid who was killed riding the wrong horse. Josie still blames herself for his death—as if she could have kept him off that horse once he put his mind to riding it. What if something happened out there...he stumbled onto something he shouldn't have? What if his death wasn't an accident, either?''

Murders...how many had there been? Reed wondered. Reba, now Peter. What about Pa? And Tucker?

Reed couldn't voice the thought. He wouldn't contemplate it, not when they'd just learned Pa could live to be ninety. And he didn't want to put any more negativity into Alcina's head about her own father, either. He prayed she was right, that Tucker and Emmett were together and safe.

"So many different kinds of bad luck here," she murmured. "How can we make sense of it all?"

Reed handed her a packet of small Post-it notes. "Use one to make a notation for each incident and the date."

He himself cleared the desk and unrolled a map of the spread on it. As Alcina scribbled down the information, he placed the Post-it in the area where the bad luck had occurred. Soon, a pattern emerged.

"Almost everything happened north of the house," Alcina said. "Mostly in the northeast quadrant to be exact."

"Where the anthrax outbreak started it all... preventing any grazing in the immediate area... stopping anyone from even going through that part of the range in fear of picking up spores and spreading them. And then the other incidents worked their way out, turning our attention farther and farther away from the original target area."

"Which was…?"

"The old silver mine."

LUNCH WAS a hurried affair. Afterward, Reed asked Felice to pack up some food for him.

"I'm going looking for varmints," he muttered.

The first Alcina had heard of it!

And when Moon-Eye showed up to collect sandwiches and drinks for himself and Frank, Reed asked him to saddle up a horse as soon as they finished eating.

That's when Alcina realized he meant to go without her.

"Make that two horses, Moon-Eye."

"Yes, ma'am."

"Whoa!" Reed said, stopping Moon-Eye from leaving. "You're not going, Alcina. You'll stay here on the ranch with Felice."

"But I plan on being with you," she sweetly insisted.

"Don't cross me on this, Alcina."

Aware that both the housekeeper and ranch hand were watching the exchange, Alcina said, "You haven't seen cross…yet. Don't try to go check out the mine area without me, Reed Quarrels."

"Or you'll what?"

"Follow you. I'll tack up a horse myself. I do know how."

Reed cursed under his breath.

Their gazes locked and Alcina was determined that she wouldn't be the one to look away. Finally, Reed caved. Alcina recognized his expression of resignation.

"Make that two horses, Moon-Eye," he said.

"Yes, sir." The hand's single good eye was sparkling.

Alcina ignored the fact that they'd provided him with his afternoon's entertainment. She had to make this right with her husband.

She touched Reed's shoulder. "Please, don't be angry. I won't hold you back. I promise."

"That's not what I'm worried about." He slid a thumb along her jawline. "I just don't want to see anything else happen to you."

"Then you'll want to keep me extra close. You won't let anything happen to me, Reed, I know that. I'd trust you with my life."

An excitement she couldn't quite put a finger on washed through Alcina. Her and Reed, riding out to the old mine together, looking for clues that would lead them to a murderer.

She shook her head. It wouldn't do to romanticize the situation.

There was nothing romantic about murder.

Then they went back to the office, where Reed sketched out a map—a blown-up version of the area they would search.

"The Silver Springs Mine has played itself out twice that I know of," he said. "What's to say someone hadn't found a new vein, just like our fathers and Noah Warner did more than forty years ago?"

Alcina was wandering around the office aimlessly as they threw the idea around.

"A new silver strike," she mused. "Wouldn't that be something? It could bring the town back to life again." Something she desperately wanted to see happen.

"More important, it could make the owner rich,"

Reed said. He folded the sketched map and set it into an inner pocket of his sheepskin jacket. "Hmm, a potential owner desperate to get his hands on the mine... Would he be desperate enough to commit murder?"

"People have killed for less."

Just then, the telephone rang and Reed answered.

"Bart, what's up?"

As Reed had mostly a one-way conversation with his brother—Reed doing most of the listening and making sounds of agreement—Alcina focused on the wall to the left of the desk. Photographs, mounted and hung, depicted the old days when the mine and town both had been thriving.

If only Main Street could be brought back to life like that, she thought.

"So what do you want me to do?" Reed asked his brother, his tone stiff. "Uh-huh."

The central photograph had been taken in front of the mine entrance. The three partners posed together, arms up around each others' shoulders. Emmett, the most commanding presence, stood in the middle. Her own father, more slightly built, and more elegant, to one side. And Noah, the obvious ladies' man with his fair good looks, to the other. All were shaved and showered and dressed in Sunday finery.

"But that's another day gone by...yeah, all right!"

Alcina glanced at Reed. He stood stiffly, his back to her, his free hand curled into a fist. As usual, he was letting his big brother run the show, whatever the show for that day might be.

Feeling his frustration from across the desk, Alcina returned her focus to the photograph. Instinct made her wish for a more detailed view. Surely a man of

Emmett's years had a magnifying glass around here somewhere.

She found a page magnifier in the first place she looked—the center desk drawer. Taking the photograph down from the wall, she set it on the desk and moved the light over it. She heard Reed hang up the phone just as she placed the magnifier over the photo.

"What are you looking for?" he asked.

"A connection..." Alcina's mouth went dry when she found one on Noah, who apparently had been quite the dandy, with a penchant for fine jewelry. "There it is!"

"What?"

She tapped the magnifier. "Come here and take a look for yourself." When he rounded the desk, she pointed to the spot. "Check out Noah's stickpin."

Reed took a good look, then turned to her. "A triangular-shaped diamond."

"Probably the same trillion-cut that Reba found."

He double-checked. "Well, I'll be..."

"So what do you think it means?" she asked, excited by the discovery.

"Hard to say. Noah Warner couldn't have anything to do with what's been going on around here—he's long dead."

"How long?"

"Since I was a kid. I remember hearing Pa talk about what a tragedy it was, but that he should have expected it."

"Expected what, exactly?"

"I don't have a clue."

"Yes, you do—right in front of you. Now, if only we could figure out how to make the connection from past to present, we might have ourselves a killer."

"We can speculate while we ride," Reed said, his tone odd, as if he was keeping something from her. "I expect you need more than what you wore here today to keep you warm, though."

He was right. The long-sleeved turtleneck and sweater-jacket and thin leather gloves were fine for a quick trip in a heated vehicle, but out in the open, she would be cold, especially since the temperature was dropping again, and there was another threat of snow. Although the down vest and Stetson hat that Reed found for her were a bit big, they would keep her warm.

And for extra protection, he added a heavy wool poncho to one of her saddlebags. Food and a flashlight already filled the other. They were ready to go.

Reed rode out on a chestnut gelding named Red Rock, while Alcina sat Feather, an Appaloosa mare.

She waited until they were well on their way to the mine, following the trail above Silverado Creek, before asking, "So, what did Bart have to say? Was it about his job?"

"No. He asked about Pa, for one, said he'd make another official report. He also got some information on the pager that was used to start the stable fire, but he expects me to sit on it until he gets home tomorrow afternoon," Reed groused. "He wanted to warn me but he didn't want me to screw up *his* case."

They were riding side-by-side, so close their legs occasionally brushed together.

Together, a beautiful word.

It was happening, Alcina thought. They were drawing closer in every way.

"What kind of information?" she asked.

"The plastic on the outside melted, the metal inside

didn't. The configuration of the boards and chips identified the manufacturer. This model turned out to be defective, the battery clip didn't hold up, so only a few hundred were manufactured. Only a few dozen were shipped to this area.''

Her pulse picked up. ''And they know who bought them?''

''Right. Because Bart went through legal channels, the lab got him a list of names and numbers, figuring he could have someone call and eliminate those in active service. But when he looked it over, Cardona jumped right out at him.''

''My God, Cesar Cardona's the one? Why didn't you say something?''

''I was thinking on it.'' Reed sounded defensive. ''Bart might be convinced, but I'm not. Too obvious. Why would a clever criminal use his own equipment when he can steal someone else's?''

''You do have a point,'' Alcina conceded. ''But what if he's not so bright? Let's just say the obvious might be right.'' She wouldn't say that Bart might be right since clearly Reed didn't want his brother to best him yet again, even if detective work was more Bart's area than Reed's. ''How would we tie Cardona back to Noah Warner?''

''Not sure. Noah's son, maybe? He's the right age. Not the right coloring, though. Noah was married to a little blonde—I remember her hair was like spun silver. But according to Pa, women of all descriptions lined up to get a shot at him, and married or not, Noah liked his extracurricular activities.''

''Last night, I asked Cardona if he ever lived in the area,'' Alcina said. ''He admitted he did for a few years, when he was a boy. And he does have a definite flare for dramatic clothing and jewelry like the Noah Warner in that photo. Do you remember at the wedding he was wearing a jeweled watch—maybe with a trillion-cut diamond in a loose setting, which would explain why he wasn't wearing the watch last night.''

''I didn't look that close,'' Reed admitted, still sounding underwhelmed.

Alcina suspected Reed wanted it to be someone else—Vernon Martell, perhaps? Or would anyone do as long as it wasn't Bart's chief suspect?

Couldn't he see that the pieces of the puzzle fit together so neatly? Alcina wondered.

Cardona…Noah's illegitimate son?

Not that she saw Noah in him. They were lightness and dark. Opposites. Cardona could look like his mother, though. And the last name could be hers. Or that of a stepfather.

Stepfather… Now, why did that ring a bell? Alcina couldn't pin the memory.

What she did remember was Cardona saying he'd waited a long time to get what he deserved. Maybe he'd wanted more of an inheritance from his father than a diamond, as costly as that one obviously was.

If it was Cardona, had he really found a new vein in the mine? she wondered. Or did he simply want what he thought was his due, worthless though it might be?

They rode along in silence for a while. Alcina let Reed set the pace. He took the horses out into a comfortable lope, their long legs eating the distance to the mine. Then they slowed. The horses blew through their noses and she saw the slight clouds they made— warm air hitting cold.

Perhaps this wasn't the best moment to bring it up, but Alcina couldn't get over the way Reed resisted Bart's notion about Cardona being the one. It jibed with the way the brothers functioned together. Hmm, the word was *dysfunctional.* She knew something of that from her own family dynamics.

Slightly behind, she goosed Feather to catch up with Red Rock.

"Reed, about the thing you have with Bart..."

He frowned at her. "Bart and I don't have a thing."

"Of course you do. It's like this silent competition that you always let him win."

"I don't know what you're talking about."

"Then you're in deep denial, Reed, because everyone around you can see it. Chance half hated Bart when he came to live on the Curly-Q because—"

"Chance loves Bart like I do. We're brothers."

"There's room for more than one emotion in the same heart. I remember how Chance was, a lot of times because of you. He was fighting your battles for you."

"I never asked him to. Besides, Bart's the oldest. He's the one Pa counts on."

"And you're just as important. And as smart. And even better at some things than he is. Like running the ranch. Bart does good, Reed, but you'd do better and you'd love running it. Bart has the heart of a lawman and that'll never change. Don't let him ruin that for himself, Reed. Don't ruin things for *your*self. Speak up before it's too late."

Chapter Twelve

Don't ruin things for yourself...speak up before it's too late.

Alcina's words still echoed through Reed's head even as they rode along. But he wasn't just thinking about his running the ranch. Uppermost in his mind was the way he was cheating her of a real marriage.

But would his speaking up about their marriage do anything but destroy the delicate fabric of the relationship they were now weaving?

Reed was at odds with himself on the matter.

He'd come to realize that Alcina was not only a lady with a heart of gold, but one with a will of iron and spirit he couldn't define. She would do anything for someone she loved, he knew... He thought she would do anything for him.

He would trust her with his life even as she would trust him with hers.

Did that mean she loved him?

The landscape had changed as they crossed the shallows of the creek toward the old mine site. They were heading for the entrance the back way, where no roads existed. Even the ranch trucks couldn't come this far into the area where natural paths twisted through rocky foothills.

"It's starting to snow," Alcina said.

"So it is."

Flakes drifted down from a sheet-white sky, but Reed guessed it would be a while before their investigation was compromised.

They emerged from a deep passage to a nearly flat area. Reed gazed hard over the acreage, eventually spotting what he'd been seeking—a definite sign of human trespass.

He turned his mount. "This way."

Alcina followed, quickly coming up alongside him. "What is it?"

He pointed to the area. "Take a good look for yourself."

"An opening in the ground."

"That's one of the old stopes. After the mine was closed down, wooden traps were used to seal all the shafts to prevent anyone from accidentally taking a fast and perhaps fatal plunge down into the tunnels."

The wood had been split apart and the remains were scattered around the opening.

"You don't think someone went down there?"

"Permanently? Doubtful. Anyone resourceful enough to get in there purposely for a look-see undoubtedly had the means to get himself back out again."

They rode on a hundred yards or so before Alcina said, "Look. The remains of a campfire."

Reed dismounted, registering anything that might indicate that someone had been out here recently. He pawed through the small pile of refuse—a few discarded cans and bits of paper and plastic from food. Nothing significant.

When he rose, his boot nicked a loose stone.

Or was it?

Reed squatted to take a better look and picked up a small hunk of what turned out to be ore with shadings of silver and white and gray.

"What?" Alcina asked, bending over next to him. "Is that what silver ore looks like?"

"Nope. Dollars to doughnuts it's molybdenum, which is used to make a type of steel. A valuable ore, actually. The big moly mine near Raton has been keeping a lot of men employed for years now."

Rising, he pocketed the sample.

"So you think someone has been here recently?" Alcina asked.

"Hard to tell. Nothing's fresh. Let's keep going to the mine entrance."

As they remounted, Reed checked the sky. The snow was coming faster now, so he pushed the horses accordingly. Within a few minutes, they came up over the mine entrance and the skeletal remains of several buildings.

Reed scanned the area for any sign of a vehicle. All seemed deserted, a true ghost town. And it was beginning to look even more ghostly as a dusting of fresh snow already covered the ground and weather-ravaged roofs.

"All clear," he said, leading the way down to the entrance level.

"Now what?" Alcina asked.

"Now we get down and take a better look on foot."

"But what exactly are we looking for?"

"Anything that would indicate recent activity."

They left the horses with reins draped over a piece of abandoned equipment halfway between the mine itself and the buildings that had been used for offices and ore processing.

The mine was a small old-time operation. The mouth set into the side of the hill had been boarded up when the mine had gone bust.

"Have you ever been inside?" Alcina asked.

"Not since I was a kid and Bart and Chance and I decided to go exploring."

"Did Emmett ever find out?"

"Yep, and Pa got wound up like a rattler. He yelled at us about how we'd fall down some stope and no one would ever find us again."

They reached the crusher, which had been used to smash the ore into smaller pieces. What was left of a broken-down and rusty conveyor led out from it to nowhere.

Reed futilely scoured the area around it for signs of recent activity.

Then he made his way toward the mine entrance. From a distance, it appeared to be sealed up tight, but as he drew closer, he noticed some of the boards seemed a little loose. Loose enough for a man to get inside?

He glanced back to share the discovery with Alcina, but she had wandered in the opposite direction, toward what was left of the rotting buildings. She stood rooted to the spot at a broken-out window.

The skin along his neck crawled.

"Reed!" Alcina's voice sounded strained. "You might want to come over here!"

Her shout was punctuated by a sharp whine, and shattered chips of wood sprayed her.

"Alcina, get to the horses now!" Reed yelled, even as a second bullet churned up the earth near her feet.

She didn't hesitate, but flew as if her life depended on it. Which it very well might, Reed knew, running as well.

Alcina was closer. She reached the horses first, grabbed Feather's reins and tossed him Red Rock's.

Reed mounted and moved out, yelling, "Follow me."

Another blast from the rifle high above him made him look behind to check on Alcina. She was halfway into the saddle when the whine of another bullet freaked Feather. The mare bolted. Her right leg raised, her body off balance, Alcina went flying and landed hard, hip first.

Reed gathered Red Rock and circled him back to her even as she managed to get herself off the ground.

Slowing, he held out his arm and hooked her just above the waist. She had the good sense to grab on to him. Under a steady barrage of bullets that whizzed by, one at a time, a few too close for comfort, he headed directly for the rear of the buildings, which offered temporary protection.

There he set Alcina down, removed a foot from the stirrup, offered her a hand and said, "Climb on up in back of me."

Breathing hard and obviously in pain, she could only nod. But after she hooked a foot in his free stirrup and bounced upward, he heard her muffled grunt. Then she was behind him, her arms securely around his waist.

Relief that she was all right washed through Reed,

but it was short-lived. They had to get out of there immediately.

Gritting his teeth, he told her, "Hold on."

Then he took off fast. Only a few bullets followed, since Red Rock took them out of rifle range in a moment.

Soon they were back in winding foothills. Unless the gunman had a horse, which Reed doubted, they were safe. He slowed to save his mount.

"How are you doing back there?"

"Fine, considering."

Grateful that she was safe, that she was pressed against his back, her arms around his middle, Reed offered up a moment of silent thanks.

Then he asked, "What was it you wanted me to see inside the building?"

"A car." Her voice grew excited. "Not a pickup or an SUV. A car. And I think it's Daddy's."

Which meant Tucker and Pa were somewhere around the mine. Or in the mine.

Or what was left of them was inside.

Reed didn't want to think too closely on the odds of whether or not the old men were still alive.

The snow was falling harder as Reed pushed out of the foothills only to catch sight of Feather grazing as if nothing at all had happened to spook her. He let Alcina down before he got to the mare, then calmly walked Red Rock right up to her. The horses were busy exchanging greetings when he grabbed Feather's reins. He held them out to Alcina.

"Can you mount by yourself?"

"I should hope so," she said, bristling before his eyes. "That wasn't the first spill I ever took."

Reed grinned. Alcina mounted with no trouble, but

he noticed that she sat gingerly, as if she was hurting more than she wanted to let on.

"We have to go back," she announced.

"To get shot?"

"Both of our fathers are in trouble. You know that as well as I do. We have to rescue them."

"We can't. I mean, not now. Everything happened so fast, I didn't even get to figure out where the shots were coming from. We'd be sitting targets."

"What do you suggest, then?"

Reed had the awful feeling that if he said, 'Go back to the house and call the sheriff,' she would return to the mine without him. Besides, he didn't really want to do that, either. It might compromise their fathers' safety…if they really were still alive.

Pa *had* to be alive, Reed thought. Nothing had ever been settled between them.

"We have to wait until later, Alcina, until it's dark and the gunman is gone or off guard."

"Gunman? You don't think it's Cardona?"

Reed shook his head. "I can't see him up in that rock, lying in wait with a rifle for some trespasser to come along. He's got other things to occupy him. He would have hired someone to do the dirty work."

Riding all the way back to the ranch house and then returning later didn't make sense. They'd be too exhausted to do anyone any good.

Besides, they could use shelter as soon as possible. The snow was coming down in a thick, wet sheet now.

Only one place he could think of to wait out the storm.

GLAD TO BE out of the blinding snow, Alcina moved to the back of the underhang where she threw down the saddlebags. The natural shelter halfway up the rimrock was a huge shallow cave of sorts, large enough to shelter not only them but the horses, as well.

While she removed Red Rock's saddle, Reed built a fire.

"Handy having firewood in here," she said.

"Bart and Chance and I have always kept firewood stacked. This was our favorite hideout ever since we were kids. Our version of a tree house."

She heaved the saddle near the leather bags on the other side of the pit and noted that Reed was already coaxing a flame to life. He grabbed a couple of bigger chunks of cedar and set them across the flame.

"Mmm, smells wonderful."

"Give it five minutes and it'll be toasty warm in here."

Alcina certainly hoped so. She fetched the second saddle. She had to admit that she was looking forward to some warmth. The wet snow had soaked through the jeans' legs and the arms of her sweater.

Moving around helped her dispel the chill. She used a saddle blanket to wipe down the horses. Feather blew through her nose and lipped Alcina's arm.

"If that's a hint for a treat, you'll have to wait until I see what Felice packed for us."

In the meantime, she scratched the horse's nose and patted her neck, then went on to Red Rock.

"So, when was the last time you were here?" she asked Reed.

"A few years back, when all three of us were home at the same time for Christmas. We rode up here on

Christmas Eve, after Pa went to bed. It was a nice, low-stress holiday. Unusual for the Quarrels family.''

"Hopefully, there'll be a lot more of them in the future.''

"Yeah, right.''

She knew he was thinking of their fathers, wondering if the men were still alive. She refused to consider the alternative. Emmett and Daddy would be all right. She and Reed would see to it.

Together, they could do anything.

With the fire now going gangbusters, Reed had turned his attention to the sitting area. He'd already lined up the saddles side by side before the fire. As she joined him, he shook out the wool cape and covered both the saddles and the ground in front of them.

"The best I can do in the way of comfort,'' he said. "Are you hungry?''

"I'm too worried to have an appetite.''

"You'd better find one. Your body is going to need fuel if you expect to pull off a rescue attempt.''

Attempt…would they succeed?

Knowing Reed was right, Alcina tried to eat. She finished most of her sandwich and some beans and rice, but merely took a bite of her apple to more easily split it. Then she gave a half to each horse and washed her hands with the snow that she scooped from the edge of the overhang.

Outside the shelter, the snow had increased to near whiteout conditions. Rather, grayout, since the hour was late. Wherever it was hiding behind the banks of clouds, the sun was setting. Another hour and it would be dark. Hopefully, the storm would let up by then.

Thinking ahead to what lay in store for them, feeling as if she'd swallowed a live snake, Alcina moved around restlessly.

"That won't do anyone any good," Reed said from the other side of the fire. "You're worrying yourself sick."

"Are you saying you're not worried?"

"I'm trying not to think too far ahead. Come on back here." He patted the area on the ground next to him. "Let's see if I can help you unwind."

Alcina didn't see any harm in a little closeness. She rejoined Reed on their makeshift seating area and didn't even protest when he began to massage her shoulders.

His touch, combined with the warmth of the fire, soon had her feeling more intimate things, albeit ones that made her equally nervous.

"Better?"

"Much," she fibbed.

But she didn't protest when he pulled her back against his chest and wrapped his arms around her waist. She closed her eyes and pretended the only thing she had to worry about was the two of them and their mixed-up relationship. That was more than enough to occupy her mind.

"Reed, there's something I need to tell you." She didn't know what else the night would hold, but it was time she was honest with him. "It's something I should have admitted to right off when you proposed. Only, everything went so fast...and then I was afraid..."

"You don't have to be afraid of me," he murmured, nuzzling the hair around her ear.

Yes, she did. She was afraid of his not being in her life. That she might drive him out for good. But he

had to know sometime. Still, she found it difficult to
get directly to the point.

"When I came home from graduate school, I was
hoping…well, you and I didn't seem so far apart in
age then, not like in high school. I—I'd always liked
you…well, more than liked you, and…"

"Just tell me."

"I was in love with you, Reed, and you were engaged to be married." He tightened his hold on her,
but she couldn't look at him. If she did, she might
not be able to continue. She laid her head back against
his shoulder. "I couldn't stand it, so I went back to
New York. I'd met Jeffrey Van Ack before, at school.
This time, he decided to sweep me off my feet…and
I let him."

"You mean that you slept with him."

"I mean that I married him."

He stiffened. "Are you telling me that you're a
bigamist?"

"No, of course not!" she protested. "We were
married for less than a year."

"Then what's the problem?"

Realizing he sounded relieved, she faced him. "I
thought you would be the one with the problem because I didn't tell you up front. But no one in town
knew, except for Pru, of course, because I didn't want
them to. I—I was so humiliated because Jeffrey—"

"Shh." He interrupted the last of it and gave her
a comforting squeeze. "It sounds to me like you're
through with Jeffrey."

"I was through with him a decade ago."

"Then why should I have a problem?"

Alcina sagged with relief. She'd been dreading this
moment for nothing. And there was no need to ex-

plain the humiliation part about Jeffrey wanting her family connections rather than her. Reed wasn't demanding a detailed explanation.

"Hey—" he tipped her chin so that she was gazing into his eyes "—you're my wife now. That's all that matters."

The way he said it made her heart race stronger. "That sounds so...so personal."

"It *is* personal," he whispered, trailing his mouth from her ear to her lips. "Very personal."

When he kissed her, Alcina's emotions unfurled inside and threatened to overwhelm her.

She turned to meet him more fully, mouth to mouth, breasts to chest. He tangled his hand in the back of her hair and tightened his hold on her as if he were branding her as his own. She'd wanted this for so long.

At last...at last...

At last he was holding her and kissing her and touching her the way she'd dreamed of so many lonely nights. There was an urgency to his seduction that thrilled her.

Was it that he'd finally realized he loved her?

Or the fact that he knew they would walk through danger together tonight?

That thought made her a little desperate. She feared not only for their fathers but for him. For them.

If something happened to Reed now...

No, she wouldn't think about that. It was all happening for her at last, and she would not allow the dark forces at work to cheat her of her due, not when she finally had what she wanted.

When Reed unzipped her vest, she did the same for him, opening his shirt to her searching touch. The feel of his warm flesh under her fingertips made her dizzy with longing. As he undressed her further, laved her neck and her breasts with warm, moist kisses, she gave in to every feeling she'd ever had for him.

He reached down into her unzipped jeans. "You're wet," he murmured into her mouth as he sank two fingers in deeper.

"I know. So what are you going to do about it?"

She was naked in a moment, but not long enough to be cold. Soon his hot body was pressed to hers. He kissed her mouth, then explored lower. He captured her nipple and tugged until it extended tight and hard and resulted in a glorious wave of pleasure.

She moaned "enough," but he didn't stop.

He licked and nipped her stomach, placed his hands on the insides of her thighs and spread her wide. Then his hands cupped her buttocks and he opened her to him like a feast that he began ravishing with tongue and teeth.

She was panting…pleading…ready to light and soar with the fire he created.

Fisting his hair, she pulled his head upward, and somehow, without any guidance he found her and slid inside. She was more than ready for him. With his first thrust, a shudder began deep inside her.

She lifted her hips to take all of him…everything he had…everything she had ever wanted from him.

And then a golden light filled her mind.

Alcina gave over to the passion she'd always dreamed of having with Reed.

But this was no dream a little voice whispered. This was the real thing.

Real flesh…joined in celebration…the dawn before the darkness to come.

REED COULDN'T GET OVER the fact that Alcina had been in love with him for years.

He'd lain awake thinking about it for the longest time with her in his arms. Eventually, he'd slept. When they'd awakened, the storm had abated and the hour had grown late. They'd ridden out by the light of the moon.

"We can leave the horses here," he said softly, stopping before they left the last of the foothills.

"So far from the mine?"

"If we ride in, we announce our arrival, maybe draw more gunfire."

The landscape shone a bluish-silver and Reed worried that they might be spotted, anyway, but there was no helping it. They weren't that far from the abandoned buildings, and they would approach from the direction opposite the mine. Stealth on foot was their best chance for success.

"All right," Alcina said, dismounting. "I trust you."

Reed cringed at the reminder of his dishonesty.

He still couldn't believe that he'd blown his chance to speak out. The perfect opportunity had presented itself when she'd told him about her first short-lived marriage. But instead of telling her about Pa's plan, he'd made love to her.

And she'd let him.

He had a lot to atone for.

They tethered their horses to a low-growing cedar.

"Can you handle this?" Reed asked of a looped rope.

Alcina took it from him and pulled it over her head and one arm so that it lay across her body. Reed himself shouldered a saddlebag heavy with flashlights and some tools that might come in handy. Lastly, he slipped the rifle from its saddle holster and prayed he'd have no cause to use it.

Prayed he'd have no cause to regret bringing her along. He'd tried not to, but once more, Alcina had threatened to follow him if he dared leave her behind.

"One moment," she said as he was about to set off. She placed her hand on his arm and lifted her head to brush her lips across his. "A kiss for luck."

"Then make it a kiss!" he breathed.

Reed pulled Alcina to him and kissed her deeply until she shuddered in his arms. Words unspoken welled in him like a storm about to break. But words would have to wait.

"No more distractions," he said, setting her from him. "We need eyes in the back of our heads."

Though she seemed uncertain, she didn't argue, merely walked by his side…a woman with her man.

When they came to the clearing where they would become vulnerable, he put an arm out and scanned every inch of the landscape before them. Nothing caught his attention. Nothing moved. Straight ahead, the abandoned hulks awaited them.

They crept as one…silently…swiftly…stopping only when they arrived at the first building, where they ducked under its shelter. A chance to catch their breath…and let their heartbeats slow.

And to check out the car up close.

"It's Daddy's," Alcina confirmed, her voice trembling with excitement.

Reed pulled a flashlight from the saddlebags and shone it inside. "No signs of a struggle."

"Is that good?"

"There's no blood," he said simply, moving to an

opening that had once been a window, where he could look across an open area to the mine entrance.

He listened hard for anything that would indicate another presence.

The howl of a coyote in the distance crept along his spine. An answer came from a different direction. Soon there was a chorus…passionate…short-lived.

Suddenly, all was still.

It was time.

"Ready?" he asked, grasping Alcina's hand.

She squeezed in answer.

It took mere seconds to flee across the open area…the longest seconds of Reed's life.

No shots rang out. No shouts of warning.

Then they were at the entrance. And the boards that had looked loose to him earlier were easily pried open, enough for them to squeeze through.

And then they were in.

Chapter Thirteen

Alcina took a shaky breath and whispered, "We did it!"

"Take this," Reed said in a low tone, pressing a flashlight into her hand. "But don't flip it on yet. Let's get away from the entrance."

Her eyes adjusted quickly to the dark. A bit of moonlight filtered through the cracks between boards and into the mouth of the mine. She could see the direction the tunnel took. And then only darkness lay beyond.

"Be careful of your footing. The mine floor can be treacherous," Reed warned her, guiding her by the arm for several yards.

Then he switched on his flashlight and aimed the beam along the wall.

"What are you looking for?"

"This." He'd pinned a piece of equipment in the bright beam. "A generator. Let's see if it's working."

A moment later, bare bulbs, strung every dozen yards or so, faintly glowed down the length of the tunnel. Minimal light, but it meant making their going easier. And they could save on flashlight batteries if necessary.

Alcina had never been inside a mine before, and this was one of the old ones, originally dug earlier in the century by a handful of men before the development of sophisticated equipment. On a slight downward incline, the tunnel was less than six feet wide and somewhere between seven and eight feet high. The support beams appeared rotted to her, and she wondered how they still held the roof from falling in. Water seeped down the walls. The floor beneath her feet was slick in spots. A thin skin of mud oozed over the metal tracks meant to convey ore cars back to the entrance.

Reed indicated a hole in the side of the wall ahead.

"That's a stope," he told her. "Men blasted and dug their way down to a lower level and sent the debris back up in an ore bucket."

He hunkered down and shone his flashlight through the ragged opening half blocked by a fallen beam. Fearing what they might find, Alcina held her breath. Debris everywhere, nearly filling the cavity.

Reed muttered, "Looks like a cave-in."

No bodies, though, at least none they could see.

Alcina shivered, but not because she was cold. The temperature was far warmer than it had been outside. Like a cave, an underground mine would keep a steady, moderate temperature all year round. She shivered because she'd never felt quite so claustrophobic.

Her uneasiness at whether or not they'd find their fathers alive growing, she followed Reed without comment. Every so often, he stopped to check an area more thoroughly for signs. Mostly what he found was that someone had been chipping away in search of new veins.

They came across another stope, in better shape than the last, but their view was partially blocked.

"Pa!" Reed yelled. "Tucker?"

"Daddy, are you there?"

Their voices echoed hollowly along the damp walls, but only someone inside the mine itself would be able to hear, she knew. Her stomach knotted at the thought.

"Nothing," Reed said.

Alcina didn't know what she had expected—Daddy and Emmett wouldn't be waiting for them at the entrance with open arms—but her sense of an impending crisis multiplied.

And her paranoia. For now she feared they weren't alone. That the villain was lurking in the shadows, waiting to surprise them, to bury them alive...

They hadn't gone very far before Reed stopped and shone his light through another low opening.

"Pa!"

"Daddy!"

"Hang on," Reed said. "This stope is clear. We're going down."

"Down?" she gasped, glancing over her shoulder into the dimness they'd left behind. "How far?"

Had she actually heard something—a foot slipping on the muck—or was her imagination playing tricks on her?

"Down to the next level and a lower tunnel."

Her heart skipped a beat and she grabbed his arm. "Reed, I'm not sure about this. What if...what if we're not alone in here?"

He turned to her and cupped her face, stroked her cheek with his thumb.

"You're spooked, I know," he said. "But we're

here now and if Tucker and Pa are still alive, we have to find them before it's too late. I'm willing to try whatever is necessary.''

''Of course. You're right.'' She pressed her face into the warmth of his palm, but that didn't dispel the uncertainty that overtook her. ''Whatever it takes.''

''Let me go first.''

She watched the tunnel behind them as he led the way down the ladder that was hooked into the side of the vertical tunnel. No movement. No sound. So why did she have this pressing sensation that they were being watched?

As she followed, she tried not to shake as the ladder moved under her weight. What was left of a pulley system dangled next to her, reminding her of how very dangerous the old mine could be. As hard as she tried to focus on the positive, she kept imagining Cesar Cardona stalking them, waiting for his chance to trap them forever…as he might already have trapped their fathers.

''You're almost there,'' Reed said from behind her.

He put his hands around her waist and helped her down. She settled back against him for a moment and he hugged her.

''C'mon, the tunnel's clear.''

The tunnel narrowed and split.

''What do we do now?'' Alcina asked.

''Check both branches, one at a time.''

''That would take forever.'' And she wanted out in the worst way. ''Let's split up.''

''No.''

''It'll be faster.''

''No.''

''Reed…whatever it takes, remember? If I find

them, I'll yell for you and you'll come running. Or you'll yell and I'll come.''

Though still reluctant, Reed agreed that her plan made sense. He gave her a swift kiss, admonished her to be careful of where she stepped, and went down the passage to the right.

Taking a deep breath, Alcina explored the tunnel to the left, checking every crevasse, and continuing to call out for her father and Emmett.

The tunnel seemed to go on forever, and just when her hope faded, she heard a faint "Over here…"

"Daddy? Emmett? I'm coming. Say something so I can find you.''

"Here…hurry…"

The voice was clearer now. Clear enough to make her stop dead in her tracks. That voice didn't belong to either of the old men.

"Alcina, over here," came the ghostly voice. "Come to Daddy."

Her skin crawled and her heart thundered so loud in her ears she almost missed the closer warning.

"No, go back…" came a weak, aged voice. "…a trick."

"Daddy!" she cried, just as the lights went out.

Pulse racing, Alcina fumbled with her flashlight, her fingers suddenly turning uncooperative. At last she switched it on and almost dropped it again when she saw the villain standing within reach of its beam.

"You!"

"Keep your mouth shut or I'll shoot," he warned her.

She stared stupidly at the gun in his hand. And when he grabbed her arm and put the metal barrel to her temple, she didn't fight him.

"Too late...too late..." came a moaning from below.

"Daddy, are you all right?" she called out.

"I told you to shut up!" He jerked her around. "But I guess you won't be satisfied unless you see for yourself. Point the flashlight down to your left."

She did as ordered.

Another opening. Another shaft. Two men, looking older than she'd ever seen them, huddled together on the floor, more than a dozen feet below.

"Are you all right?" she asked again.

"See for yourself, bitch."

With that, her captor gave her a sharp shove.

Alcina screamed as she flew forward, her stomach dropping faster than the rest of her. She landed directly on top of her father and Emmett. They sprawled across the floor in a tangle of arms and legs and loops of the rope that had fallen free from her body.

"Sweetheart, are you all right?"

"Daddy," she cried, righting herself. If she was hurt, she'd figure it out later. "Thank God the two of you are alive."

"Not for long," Emmett muttered darkly. "You, neither. My fault. Never should have involved you. For once, I should have kept my nose where it belonged."

"What are you talking about?" Alcina asked. "It's not your fault that we came looking for you instead of leaving it to the authorities."

"I didn't know it would come to this," Emmett protested weakly. "I didn't know that I would put your life in danger when I made Reed marry you."

"You made Reed marry me?" a stunned Alcina echoed. He'd told her to think of it as a business deal…but this? Unthinkable! Only, she had to know. "What do you mean?" she demanded. "How? Why?"

Sounding like a man doomed by his own hand, Emmett said, "I guilted him into it to save the ranch…but it was already too late."

ALCINA'S SCREAM raised the hair on Reed's neck and arms.

Without giving it a second thought, he dropped the saddlebag off his shoulder and raced down the tunnel, rifle in one hand, flashlight in the other. He had to get to her—she must have hurt herself in the dark. He should have known that old generator wouldn't be reliable.

He slowed as he reached the split in the tunnel and shifted gears to enter the other branch.

"Alcina!" he cried. "Say something, sweetheart! I'm coming for you!"

He heard a scuffle directly ahead. His flashlight beam hit not his wife, but a hulk of a man. Staring into the barrel of a gun, Reed stopped and fought for breath.

"Well, ain't that sweet? You're just in time to die with your loved ones. Drop the rifle, Quarrels."

The man grinned but the smile didn't reach his pale eyes. His silver buzz cut gleamed in the darkened tunnel. So they'd been wrong about Cardona, Reed thought, taking inventory.

Hugh Ruskin was standing next to an opening. Had he thrown Alcina down that shaft?

A fist closed around Reed's heart, and he feared he was already too late. He dropped the rifle.

"Ruskin, where are they?"

"Ah, so anxious." The bartender flicked on a miner's light that he'd attached to his jacket. "Don't worry, they're all still alive. You'll have time for a last goodbye. Now kick that rifle over here."

Reed nearly collapsed with relief. Anything was still possible, then. He kicked the rifle just short of the other man. The bartender waved the gun as if Reed should start walking, but Reed wasn't in a co-operative mood.

"You won't get away with this."

Ruskin moved closer, stepping over the rifle. "You're mistaken, Quarrels. My father might have been a weak man, but I suggest you don't underestimate *me*. Your pa and Tucker Dale forced him out of their partnership for a pittance, but I intend to reclaim my rightful inheritance."

Reed thought he heard a thunk somewhere behind Ruskin. Not knowing who was back there or what the person was up to, Reed decided to keep the bartender talking and distracted.

"Your father? Your father was Noah Warner?" Reed asked. "Noah sold out. You have no claim to the mine."

"His partners cheated him!" Ruskin boomed. "And when he lost what they gave him gambling, he ate a gun, leaving my mother and me to fend for ourselves. Noah Warner's legacy consisted of a lousy diamond stickpin and a silver ring he had made from the first piece of ore he brought out of this mine. I'll bet your pa never told you that my father was the one who found the new vein in the first place. Just like I found the vein of molybdenum that'll make me as rich as I deserve to be."

"So you were behind all the bad-luck incidents on the Curly-Q, starting with the anthrax outbreak?"

"You figured that out. You're smarter than I thought. And with the Curly-Q on the auction block I would have gotten my hands on it all. I have friends with deep pockets and a taste for big profits."

"Tell me, Ruskin, what did Peter Dagget and Reba Gantry ever do to you?"

"They got in the way. Just like you." Ruskin pulled something from his pocket. "But I intend to fix it so no one finds any of you unless they dig up a couple of tons of rock."

Ruskin was holding a cell phone.

Reed's mouth went dry. He'd bet dollars to doughnuts that a pager was wired nearby. And this time it wouldn't be set to start a fire.

Reed was certain that Ruskin had hooked the damn thing up to sticks of dynamite that could blow them all to kingdom come.

"TRY AGAIN, Emmett!" Alcina urged, aiming the flashlight beam upward. "You can do it!"

Looped rope in hand, Emmett whirled it around his head and let it free. It flew straight up to the mechanism controlling the ore bucket that was stalled at the top of the shaft. This time it held.

"Good job." Her plan was working already. She handed him the flashlight so he could use it to guide her. "I'm ready, Daddy."

Alcina waved her father to the wall.

That the old men were down here was her fault. Daddy had recognized the diamond, and when Emmett had accused him of being responsible for the Curly-Q's troubles, Daddy had shoved the thing in his face. Emmett had remembered seeing Noah's silver ring on the bartender at Chance's wedding, but it hadn't registered then.

Together, the men had lain in wait for Ruskin, who had in turn trapped them in the mine.

The bastard had bragged about how he'd shot at her and Reed when they'd come poking their noses around the mine earlier. Alcina supposed he got some perverse pleasure in trying to break their spirits.

But both men had plenty of spirit left.

Her father gave Alcina a leg up. She latched onto the rope, braced her free foot against the wall and half pulled, half climbed her way up, inches rather than feet at a time.

"That's it," her father whispered encouragingly. "You've almost got it, sweetheart."

Her arms burned, her fingers stung, her legs protested wildly. She stalled out a few feet from the top to catch her breath and to find her reserve of energy.

"Only a little farther," Emmett urged.

Alcina heard other voices, too—faint but not too far away—Reed arguing with Ruskin. No doubt the bastard had the drop on her husband and would soon force him to join the party.

She figured she didn't have much time.

Clenching her jaw against the pain, she managed the last few feet and grabbed the heavy steel ore bucket that was big enough to hold a person. The bucket gave unexpectedly and Alcina cried out as her feet swung away from the wall. She hung on fiercely and waited for it to settle back against the rock.

Then she clambered up onto the tunnel floor.

"Shine the light up here," she whispered.

She needed to see what she was doing. While the

pulley system was normally run by generator, Emmett had told her it could be operated manually in case of power failure. The men would attempt to come up in the bucket, one at a time, using their own combined strength to work the pulley cables. She released the brake and carefully lowered the bucket.

Now it was up to them to get themselves out. She had to do something to even the playing field with Ruskin.

Crouching in the dark, she felt around the slime-covered floor for something she could use as a weapon. Daddy had told her he'd seen some handheld mining tools against the opposite wall. Her fingers nicked a length of metal—one of the rods a worker drove into the rock to make a niche for explosives. It was long, she estimated three feet, and heavy.

Drawing on strength she wouldn't have bet she still had, Alcina lifted the drill rod. She glanced down the shaft to see how the men were doing. Daddy was in the ore bucket and he and Emmett were using the pulley system to inch him up.

No time to wait.

Weapon balanced in both hands, she crept forward and prayed for a clear shot at the man who would see them all dead.

"LOOK, we can fix this like reasonable men."

Reed was stalling for time. He'd sworn he'd seen movement beyond the rim of his light.

"What if I don't want to be reasonable?"

"You want to be rich, right? And wouldn't you rather do that without the law looking over your shoulder?"

"You mean your brother?"

Reed was hoping for an opening to rush the bartender, but Ruskin wasn't giving him one.

"Bart won't take our deaths lightly. And he'll know, when you try to buy the property—"

"Ah, stuff it! I can take care of him if I need to. *And* your little brother—"

"Ee-yah-ah!"

The scream cut through Ruskin's words and took him off guard. He swung around, gun hand first. Even as Reed rushed forward, Alcina swung a long metal rod and whomped his arm.

Ruskin screamed, "Bitch!" as both gun and cell phone went flying. They skittered along the slippery floor.

Reed was flying, too. He tackled the bastard, and they rolled, Reed landing beneath the bigger man, who elbowed him hard.

"Reed!" Alcina screamed.

"Stay away," he managed to grunt, fearing Ruskin might hurt her.

The breath was knocked out of him, but as Ruskin started to get up, Reed managed to hook a foot around the bartender's ankle. The man pitched forward, landing on hands and knees.

A temporary reprieve.

Ruskin was up on his feet in seconds. Spinning, he kicked out at Reed who rolled again, narrowly avoiding the boot.

Then Ruskin made a dive for the ground.

The rifle!

Reed flew for it, too.

Both men locked hands on the weapon at the same time. Ruskin was bigger. Stronger. But Reed had wrestled thousands of calves to the ground to brand them. Leverage was everything. He let go of the rifle and grabbed on to Ruskin's leg and gave it an expert twist and jerk.

With a yell, the bartender toppled.

Reed watched as, seemingly in slow motion, the rifle flew one way, Ruskin the other...making a perfect dive over the precipice and straight down the shaft.

His protracted scream raised the hair along Reed's neck.

"Son, are you all right?"

Reed managed to get himself to his feet. "Pa! Thank God." The old man looked exhausted, but he was moving fine. Reed clapped him on the back.

"Sweetheart, you did it," Tucker said, hugging his daughter.

"We all did it, Daddy."

Reed picked up his flashlight and moved the beam along the floor. "The cell phone, where the hell is it?"

"You want to make a call now?" Pa asked.

"We've got to find it!" Reed said, knowing the danger was not yet over.

"It went down the shaft," Alcina told him, her voice cold enough to chill him.

He met her frosty gaze. His heart plummeted. *She knew.* Not that it would matter if they didn't get out of there and fast.

"The cell phone is down in the same stope with Ruskin?"

"I don't think he's going to call anyone for help," she told him.

"Let's get out of here, *now!*" He couldn't stress the word enough.

"You're not the boss of me, Reed Quarrels."

"Argue with me later, Alcina!" He latched on to her wrist and pulled, yelling to their fathers, "Hurry if you want to get out of here with your lives!"

They were right behind him and Alcina, who'd quit struggling against him for the moment.

Reed's heart was in his mouth as he took them back the way they'd come. His gut told him they had to get up a level and fast.

He shoved Alcina onto the stope ladder, then Pa and Tucker.

He came up last, yelling, "Keep going! Don't stop for anything!"

Apparently, his urgency had gotten through to them all. They moved faster than was safe. Tucker slipped once, but Alcina merely grabbed her father's arm to steady him and pull him faster.

They were halfway down the tunnel toward the entrance—still some distance away—when a blast thundered from behind them so strong that the support timbers began to shake and dance.

"Keep going. Faster!"

Loose rock and clouds of dust rained down on them, but the walls and ceiling held.

But Reed could sense the tunnel below collapsing…

Hugh Warner Ruskin had made certain that he would never be separated from his inheritance again.

"THANK GOD WE ALL MADE IT!" Tucker cried fervently as the four straggled out of the mouth of the tunnel.

"Thank God," Reed echoed, his gaze devouring Alcina. "You're not hurt?"

"My bruises probably have bruises." She shrugged. "I'll live."

She gave him a minute to say something more. To take her in his arms and tell her how much he loved her and how much she meant to him, but he stood there. Staring. Silent. Vintage Reed.

She looked away and murmured, "Maybe you'd better see to your father."

"Pa?"

The word came out strangled, like Reed had just remembered his father's heart. Even if the old man wasn't exactly dying, he needed care. But, to her surprise, her own father was already seeing to Emmett. Reed was sort of a third wheel in the situation. Tears sprang to her eyes as she followed, watching Reed's father lean on his old business partner.

Reed glanced back at her, his expression conveyed nothing.

Business partner...

The words echoed in her mind and Alcina couldn't shake them. Not when Reed wasn't talking to her. He was so silent.

So stiff.

So over.

And it had hardly even begun....

AFTER A NIGHT of tossing and turning, interrupted by bouts of hot tears, Alcina dragged herself out of bed knowing what she had to do.

First she needed a shower to let the steaming water beat some of the soreness out of her and some common sense into her. Not that the water could heal her emotions the way it could her body.

She missed Reed.

She would always miss him.

At least she had a few memories to keep her warm, she thought. Reed hadn't faked the passion they'd shared during the snowstorm. And she was pretty certain he was fond of her in his own way.

And in his own convoluted way, he had been truthful with her, she supposed, while she'd been purposely stupid not to understand what he'd meant by a business deal.

Well, he'd get what he'd wanted out of the marriage.

The night before, she'd dropped off Emmett and Reed at the pickup still parked behind the gas station. Reed had begged her to let him come by the bed-and-breakfast after he took his father home. He'd wanted to talk to her privately. She'd refused.

Alcina didn't want an apology from him. All she wanted was what she couldn't have—his heart.

After watching Reed drive out of her life, she'd made Daddy promise to work out a deal about the mortgage. He'd been happy to agree. It seemed that being confined and facing death together had helped him and Emmett work out their differences.

Daddy had already called over to the Curly-Q earlier this morning to learn that Bart was coordinating the official investigation. He'd decided to stay in Silver Springs and had accepted an offer arranged by his old friend, Sheriff John Malone, to be a deputy in this neck of the woods.

And, after telling her that, he'd headed over to the ranch himself to have a serious talk with all the Quarrels men.

Well, now Reed could be rid of her.

Alcina threw on her old robe and stuffed her feet

into her fluffy slippers. A look in the mirror made her shudder. But what did it matter? She was alone now.

Maybe a pot of coffee would give her the energy she needed to get through the day. She didn't know if she would ever feel like eating again.

But when she opened the bathroom door, Alcina froze in shock at the unexpected sight before her. A blanket of fresh flowers covered her bed.

And Reed was beneath them!

"What are you doing here?" she choked out, mentally ordering her racing pulse to behave.

"Sharing your bed."

She laughed bitterly. "Your services are no longer required, Reed."

"Alcina, don't talk like—"

"I'm making an appointment with a lawyer to start divorce proceedings."

"You're what?" he demanded, sitting straight up.

He was nude at least to the waist...

Alcina made a choking sound and backed up another step. She should slam the bathroom door and lock it until he left.

"Alcina, do you love me or not?"

"My heart's not the one in question."

"You know how I've always had trouble speaking up for myself—well, I told Pa and Bart that I'm the man to run the spread. And they both agreed."

"I'm happy you settled things with your family."

"You are my family now, Alcina. I should have spoken out to you yesterday when I realized this..." He took a deep breath as if searching for his courage. "My heart is already yours."

Alcina swallowed hard. Reed wouldn't lie to her, would he? Not directly, at least.

"What are you saying, Reed Quarrels?"

"That I love you, Mrs. Quarrels, and I want to stay married to you and to make babies with you."

Everything she'd wanted to hear him say…

The only protest she could find was "What if we can't? Make babies, that is. I am older than you and it might not be so easy."

"Then we'll keep trying," Reed said seriously. "I'm a very hard worker, in case you haven't realized it."

While he wore a poker face, Alcina knew he was teasing her.

Spirits soaring as she realized her dream was finally coming true, she asked, "What are you wearing under all those flowers?"

He grinned. "Why not come here and find out for yourself?"

Epilogue

Emmett was quite pleased with himself as he dressed for Barton and Josie's wedding. Lainey and Daniel couldn't be happier to get a new mother. The new year sure was starting out right. He grinned as he buttoned his shirt and slipped on a string tie.

The Quarrels family had turned into something!

His boys had pooled their resources to make the back mortgage payments. And they'd leased away the mineral rights to the northeast quarter of the property for the next ten years to keep the Curly-Q in the black.

The mortgage up-to-date.

Silver Springs flourishing—houses and stores in town being fixed up for the new mine workers.

Barton running the town, Reed running the ranch, and Chance not running at all anymore.

Not with that rodeo school Chance and Josie were planning to start this summer, Emmett thought, admitting the idea had some merit after all. As did the other new-fangled ideas his sons were tossing around. He guessed he'd better listen up and let them think they were really running things. After a lifetime of resentment and disagreement, Barton, Reed and Chance were of one mind, ready to work together, to do whatever was necessary to save the family legacy.

They were finally acting like brothers should.

Emmett could bust his buttons with pride...all his scheming had paid off.

Three sons and three grandchildren and counting—he'd noticed a special smile around Alcina's mouth when she didn't think anyone was looking. A renewed friendship with his old partner Tucker. And then there was Felice, the woman who had stuck by his side no matter what his faults were. He had plans for her, too, but he'd have to be extra cagey, if he didn't want to scare her off before he got a ring on her finger.

Emmett had never felt so lucky, not even when he'd struck it rich so many years ago.

His family around him and thriving.

What more could a man ask for?

HARLEQUIN®

I N T R I G U E ®

presents

LOVERS UNDER COVER

Dangerous opponents, explosive lovers—
these men are a criminal's worst nightmare
and a woman's fiercest protector!

A two-book miniseries
by RITA Award-nominated author

Carly Bishop

They're bad boys with badges, who've
infiltrated a clandestine operation. But to
successfully bring down the real offenders,
they must risk their lives to defend the
women they love.

In April 2000 look for:

NO BRIDE BUT HIS (#564)
and
NO ONE BUT YOU coming soon!

Available at your favorite retail outlet.

HARLEQUIN®

Makes any time special ™

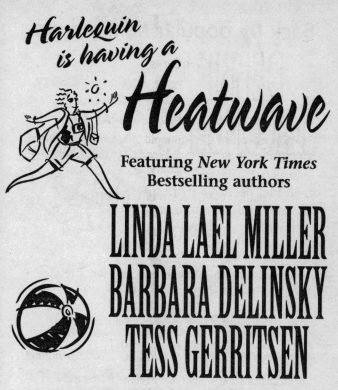

HARLEQUIN®
Makes any time special ™

HARLEQUIN®
AMERICAN ◆ ROMANCE®

WANTS TO SEND YOU
HOME FOR THE HOLIDAYS!

AmericanAirlines®

LOOK FOR CONTEST DETAILS
COMING NEXT MONTH IN ALL
HARLEQUIN
AMERICAN ROMANCE®
SERIES BOOKS!

OR ONLINE AT
www.eHarlequin.com/homefortheholidays

For complete rules and entry form send a
self-addressed stamped envelope (residents of
Washington or Vermont may omit return postage)
to "Harlequin Home for the Holidays Contest
9119 Rules" (in the U.S.) P.O. Box 9069, Buffalo,
NY 14269-9069, (in Canada) P.O. Box 637,
Fort Erie, ON, Canada L2A 5X3.

HARHFTH1